OXFORD
POLYTECHNIC
LIBRARY

D1145140

A PARCEL OF PATTERNS

JILL PATON WALSH

A PARCEL
OF PATTERNS

KESTREL BOOKS

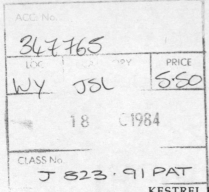

ACC. No.
347765

LOC   COPY   PRICE
WY   JSL   5.50

18   C1984

CLASS No.
J 823 . 91 PAT

KESTREL BOOKS
Published by Penguin Books Ltd
Harmondsworth, Middlesex, England

Copyright © 1983 by Jill Paton Walsh

All rights reserved. No part of this publication may
be reproduced, stored in a retrieval system, or transmitted
in any form or by any means, electronic, mechanical,
photocopying, recording, or otherwise, without the prior
permission of the Copyright owner.

First published in 1983

ISBN 0 7226 5898 2

Printed in Great Britain
by Richard Clay (The Chaucer Press) Ltd
Bungay, Suffolk

Filmset in Palatino by
Northumberland Press Ltd, Gateshead

BRITISH LIBRARY CATALOGUING IN PUBLICATION DATA

Paton Walsh, Jill
A parcel of patterns.
I. Title
823'.914 [F]   PZ7

ISBN 0-7226-5898-2

For Ethel and Paul, Jane and Bill,
Betty and Alvin:
the author's Other England

A parcel of patterns brought the Plague to Eyam. A parcel sent up from London to George Vicars, a journeyman tailor, who was lodging with Mrs Cooper in a cottage by the west end of the churchyard. This was the common report and credence among us, though I heard later that the Plague was at Derby at the time when it reached us, being brought thither by a Lordship and a Ladyship fled out of London in vain hope of their own safety. Yet though Derby is the greatest town in our country of Derbyshire, it is many miles distant from Eyam; and certain it is that the parcel of patterns did come up to George Vicars, and that it was he who opened it.

Mrs Cooper was the widow of a lead-miner, killed when his pick touched off an explosion of slickensides, in a vein under Eyam Edge. She had two sons, both too young to work his title after him, so she thought good to give house and hearth room to George Vicars, first in exchange for new attire for herself and her boys, and later for money, when he should begin to be paid for his skill by other Eyam folk.

He was a bird-boned man, with a strange lolloping gait, brought about, we said – for we young folk all laughed over him – by sitting so long cross-legged on Widow Cooper's flag-door, plying his needle. He was quick-footed as he was quick-fingered, walking nowhere that he might run. He neither went to church on Sunday, nor walked up the village to Furnesses' house, where the Friends met, yet when his box was opened on his first coming to the

Coopers' there were four books in it, besides the threads and needles of his trade, and his spare shirt and stockings: a book of sermons, a Bible, and two others. Mrs Cooper, who told my mother this, could not read, and could not say what the t'others were.

There was work enough in Eyam for a tailor's needle. While the Parliament was in London, or the Lord Protector, and Parson Stanley was our parson, we were kept in sober array, and taught to think it sinful to wear frills and colours. But now the King was back, and we had a new young parson, who wore lace at his cuffs himself and preached not against tucks and dyestuffs. There were many of us wanting new garments for the Wakes.

'How will your lodger fare when the Wakes are come and gone?' my mother asked Mistress Cooper.

'It was not the Wakes that brought him here, but the fame abroad of Squire Bradshaw's new hall building,' said Mistress Cooper. 'There will be menservants and maidservants enough in such a household, and the Squire must find them all in raiment.'

Bradshaw Hall was then in the building, stone upon stone, and there were as yet no servants there, but masons and carpenters only, in dusty homespun. And so the first of the gentlefolk of Eyam to resort to George Vicars for apparel were not the Squire his kin, but Catherine, the pretty young wife of the new parson, William Momphesson. She was as fresh as a Lent lily, with a bush of red-gold hair that ever escaped her cap, and though she had borne two children she was as slender as a slip of willow. She had lived in Durham, far off, and visited London ere ever she came with the parson to Eyam, and she had a desire for fine dresses greater than other folk. She misliked all the gowns George Vicars could show unto her, and she stood – so Mistress Cooper told my mother – barefoot before the fire, spinning on the balls of her feet, looking this way and that into the glass the tailor held up to her, with a bale of blue silk thrown around her, and asked him if he had skill to cut clothes after the London fashion.

He told her he had not been in London since the coming home of the King, and had never seen the Queen and her foreign ladies, what they were wearing, but that if she would be patient he would write to a brother tailor in London for patterns of the new clothes, and as for skill to make them, once he had patterns, no tailor in England could show a neater seam ... So she disrobed herself of his bolt of silk, and said,

'I pray thee, then, send to London, Goodman Vicars.'

He wrote the letter with his own hand, and dispatched it by walking the eight miles to Chatsworth, and paying a man of the Duke of Devonshire to take it for him, he being bidden to London shortly.

Mistress Cooper was much given to standing at her gate and gossiping to those who came past for water at the river, so that Catherine Momphesson's new gown was of common report within the day. We looked to see her wear it at the Wakes; and we feared it no more than do the silly birds fear, who sing upon the ash-tree boughs.

The parcel had it never been sent for, Eyam had known never its dreadful fame. Among all places in the Low Peak it is for sure the prettiest, the softest nesting in its fold of hill, the best watered, the best lit – for the slope of Eyam Edge faces south into the sun, and the town of Eyam is along a curving street, winding on a wide ledge half way up the slope, crossed with brooks descending, and basking in the sun. Middleton folk, I know, find words to say for Middleton; but I am of Eyam, one of the four hundred and some souls of this place, and you may keep Middleton, and all places else, for me!

At Eyam we have pasture enough, but our fields are poor arable, a hard and stony soil, giving less wheat for our labour than other folk have of theirs on better land. Yet good livings have been and will be got in Eyam, because of

9

the veins of lead which underlie the place. The lead is sometimes got with sore labour, and scantily; sometimes more possibly and plentifully, but won always at hazard of men's lives. The miners live by their own laws, with bargains called lot and cope, and a Barmaster who oversees all, assigns rights in veins to who first found them out, and sees to the paying of dues, according to ancient customs. Many of the Eyam men are miners, fathers and sons; the keeping of a cow and growing salats in the cottage garths they leave to women, together with spinning and weaving, and keeping house. The mineral time of day is from seven of the morning till four of the afternoon, and for that time you will see no men in Eyam streets, but it be the smith, or the Squire, or the old men sitting in their doorways to the sun, or one of the parsons.

I see now that for this task of writing I have undertaken I lack wit and skill, and set things down awry. For Catherine Momphesson, her dress, is already written here, and how she came to Eyam is yet to be set down. But then it is no matter if it be disordered, like enough, so long as all is told.

So then, at the time of the parcel, of parsons we had two. Parson Stanley had been with us many years, longer than I can remember otherwise. But older folk well remembered a time before him, when we had had a wicked parson, who had sorely vexed the people, and at last departed, leaving no one here to christen or to marry, or to pray over the dead. Then a number of the men of Eyam agreed together, and fetched Thomas Stanley to be our parson, and petitioned Mr Saville, in whose gift the living lies, that he might consent to have Stanley, and he agreed. All this was many years before my birth, but here I set down the history of it as I had it from John Stanley, Parson Stanley's son, with whom I have played catch-and-tag all round the churchyard wall, and who grew to man's estate as one among all the boys of Eyam.

All the while from the death of the old King to the coming

home of the new, while Parliament or the Protector Crom-
well ruled the land, we had a sober and a godly church in
Eyam. Parson Stanley preached to us with the wisdom of a
Puritan, though he spoke but shortly on hellfire and at
length on God's pain at men's sins. He let the Eyam custom
still be kept of dressing the wells with pictures made of
flowers all pressed in clay, so be it that it was a picture from
the Bible that we made. Nor did he preach against the
Wakes – our Eyam has Wakes famous in all the country
round about – so be it that there was no maypole, and no
ribbons and frippery for the holiday, and no dances but of
boy with boy and girl with girl – lads' morris and lasses'
morris, divers sides of the street. I never heard of any one in
any affliction, from the richest to the poorest he, who had
not comfort from Parson Stanley. But then the times
changed.

And Parson Stanley would not use the Old Prayer Book,
now brought back, nor wear a surplice, not in church nor
street, nor have cloth upon the altar, nor a cross, nor would
he bid us bow upon the name of Jesus, for he said these
things smelt of idolatry and he could not make himself
conformable. Because of new laws about these matters he
was in danger. Some of the older men went about to persuade him to these things, for they feared that if he did not
conform we should have the wicked parson back. And this
far at least they went with him, that on Saint Bartholomew's Day, the year of Our Lord 1664, he did not depart
above ten miles from us, as the new law required him, but
leaving the parsonage he removed himself and his household across the street, and a little westwards of the churchyard, to a small house given him by a well-wisher, and
there he dwelt, being sustained at the expense of many of
the Eyam folk, who would not see him go.

It was the end of September before the new parson came
to us. A mist hung all about the hills and uplands, and out
of the mist a fine rain falling fast. The leaves were turning,

11

and the coming winter laid a chill upon the air. Allot Torre, and Ann Trickett, and Mary Gregory, and some others had lit fires in the parsonage, and laid clean rushes on the floors, in expectation of the parson's coming, and the day long we awaited him, lingering in doorways in despite of the wet, to hearken for sound of horse or cart. By night they had not reached us; and though there were voices asking what might have become of them, and wondering if they were lost upon the road, or rain-pelted, standing by a cart with a wheel come off, or suchlike mishap, we soon had our minds on nearer things, for the rain coming on very fast, the bank that holds a pool of water by the streetside over-brimmed, and made a flood across the street. A fast fresh stream runs down there, that the old women call the 'ever-water', but we younger call the river; and there is a basin made by damming the flow with an earthbank, to make a depth for dipping buckets. The overflow ripped through the bank, and spilled forth water, mud and slime into the street, and set folk running hither and yon with lanterns and with spades, trying to throw dams across doorways and dig a channel for the filth to flow harmlessly away by the stocks, and not into our houses. The parsonage was all forsaken, with none to mind and mend the fires, and while we were thus beset the parson came riding up with his wife set on the saddle before him.

He had a wide plain countenance, with a big nose, and yet with not enough features for so large a face, and his hair was fair and long to his shoulders. He dismounted, and with care reached up to her, and helped her to the ground. She looked around her at the mud-bolted men standing all in the rain, and at the glint of mud and water in the street. She shrank to his side and said, quite softly – but the mist that mutes the rainsound lets all be heard – 'Oh, dearest, what a place is this!'

It was Mary Gregory who found her tongue, and saying, 'Come, my duck; come, Sire,' led them under their roof, and saving the starving fire from its last embers, made them a blaze. My mother brought a hot posset, and Allot a pan to warm the bed, and the parson, seeing off their help, said he would see his wife warm and to bed himself.

Then the women all gathered in Mrs Cooper's cottage, hard by, and talked of her – how pretty and how thin – and of him, and how his boxes and his children were waiting better weather to come from Matlock . . .

'Poor gentleman, to come by such a soaking,' Allot said.

And my mother said, 'Why, he may be wet and dry and take no harm, surely; but she hath the wasting sickness.'

'Fie, Mary, no,' said Ann. 'It is but that she is gentle-born, and not so ox-boned as we.'

'Mark me; she hath consumption,' mother said. And of this talk I had none need to tell me, for I was there. The new parson's name was William Momphesson, and his wife was Catherine, for whom the dress-patterns were fetched.

There was a thin sunlight on the morrow, by which the parson's boxes and his children came up the road. They came early, and few folk were abroad to see them come. When later we learned they would call upon the Squire, the street was thronged with folk to see them pass. The children were but babes, a girl-child just walking, holding hard to her father's hand and he stooping to reach her grasp, and a stout lad a little older, whom Mistress Momphesson was carrying till Parson Momphesson bid her set him upon his feet.

'Thou canst walk, George,' the parson said. ''Tis but a step.' For the Rectory was at the eastern side of the church-yard, and the Squire was lodged at the Talbot Inn, opposite the lych-gate, while his hall was rising to its roof.

'It is cold here,' said little George.

'This land is high, and often cold,' I said – for I was among those many standing by. 'You shall have snow every winter.'

'What! Can I sled and skate?' the boy said, stopping on his way, and turning to look on me.

'You shall borrow my sled, young master, when the snow lies deep as your middle finger is long,' I said.

For this promise I was rewarded with a sweet smile from the child's mother.

'Give the girl thanks, George, if you would have her remember that promise,' she said.

The boy blushed, and lisped a thanks with good grace enough. But his thanks were lost in a little stir and murmur going among the throng of curious bystanders; for the parson, having led his daughter as far as the threshold of the Inn, stopped there, and took off her worsted cloak, which covered her tiny person to her toes. And underneath the child was clad in crimson silk, with a wide collar all of lace. Her sleeves were slit and puffed, her sash was crusted with a pearly pattern sewn on in beads.

Many years of Parson Stanley's preaching had marked our minds with a way of thinking about garments such as that. The child was dressed in a fashion fitting for a whore!

The runners of my sled were rusted deep. I took it from behind the barrels in the yard, and rubbed it with a grit-stone to bring it clean. It was not like to snow soon, but I was happy, scraping at the rust, and remembering what the sled called into my mind. Many years since, when I was a lass of but eight or so summers, we had all gone up, pulling the sled behind us. It was a late snow, a snow of April, all frozen out of time. There is often a dusting of snow up here in April, even into May, but that year there was more than a foot deep, fallen in fearful storms, swept into great drifts, and cold-locked for many days with no thaw in prospect. A grief to our elders, and a game of sled to us. We went not up Eyam Edge, above the town, for that is fierce steep, but we went up Eyam Vale, to where the land rises at the head of the valley, onto a wide and rolling upland. This place is still within the parish and Liberty of Eyam, though there are two hamlets there with their own names – Foolow and Bretton, and a farm called Shepherd's Flat. There we looked to find a gentle slope, where we might romp in safety, being timid in our tender years. And there was Alice Sydall, and Emmot Sydall, and Ann Trickett, and Francis Archdale, and John Stanley, and Abel Coale, and Randol Daniel, and Mary Gregory, all being children of Eyam.

The snow lay thick upon the land, so that we shaded our eyes against the brightness of the uplands. Frost had crusted it, and gemmed its crunchy skim, and it was good for sledding, but hard on our hands, taking it to ball and throw. We laughed, and tumbled off the speeding sled. The boys pulled the sled along, and we pelted each other with snow. Our voices melted into miles of distance, like the snow scraps melting on our hands, raw-red with cold. Randol had brought a hot coal in a little keeping-pot of clay, and this we passed round from one to another, and cradled to comfort our freezing fingers; and Mary Gregory's mother had given us a flagon of hot broth in a pack of hay, which kept warm enough to be good to sup a gullet full, and we shared that round us too.

And while we were standing thus, passing the flagon round, we saw a stranger coming towards us. The stranger was coming from the south, and he appeared as a blinding black shadow against the snow-light off the ground. We all fell silent and watched. He still came on, making so straight a course towards us across the plain, we were no doubt his aim. He was wearing a sheepskin coat, and a hat with a wide, wide brim, and making his way upon snow-shoes, with the aid of a long staff. When he drew nearer we could see the staff was a crook. And when he came right up to us, we could see he was a young lad, in the first pride of full growth, with bright blue eyes, and a wide forehead under his wide brim.

'We don't know you,' said Ann Trickett.

'I am from Wardlow, near by,' the young man said, 'and you, I think, are from Eyam.'

'That we are, and we have no need of thee!' said Francis Archdale, who till the stranger came head and shoulders above him had been most near a man's height among us, and easily the tallest.

'Nay, surely, but I have need of you,' he was answered. 'My name is Thomas Torre. I am cousin to Torres in Eyam, and to Torres in Middleton. Fear me not.'

'Who spoke of fear?' said Francis, in a rage.

'And what do you want of us?' asked Abel.

'I have a ewe in sore distress, over yonder,' Thomas said, 'and I am loth to lose her, for she is a good beast. But what must be done, I cannot do for her myself. Give me your hands, cousins . . .'

He stretched out and took Abel's hand, and let it free the same instant, to take Ann's, and Mary's next. Emmot's he could not try, for she put them behind her back, and would not let him. But when he came to me, and took my hand, he held it longer, and spread my fingers out along the palm of his. His was wide and big, with great bony knuckles, hard and square, and against his mine was slender and short, and curled with cold.

'Thou art the one, little maid,' he said to me, 'if thou wilt, to save me my ewe and lamb. Thy hand is small enough.'

'She goes not with thee on any errand, without I go too,' said Francis. 'What do we know of thee, of sure knowledge?'

'So be,' said Thomas. 'Get on the sled behind her, and come both with me. And I will return you here within the hour.'

'We must be home by dark,' I said.

'That you shall,' he answered, and bending his strength he drew the sled behind, going over the snow the way he had come.

The ewe lay in a snowdrift into which Thomas had dug to

16

find her. His spade lay beside the broken surface, and the ewe in a brown-stained melt-smoothed cavern, from which he had taken off the roof. From her hind-parts the hooves of the lamb were thrust forth, visible. Thomas lifted me down into the snow-pit with him, and told me that the head and forefeet should come together, the nose of the lamb well down, as though it dived into the air, like a boy into a rock pool in the summer. He asked me to push the feet back, and reach in and press the head down, and make it come so. I shuddered, and put my hands behind my back.

'I cannot bear to,' I said, in a small voice.

'She will die, if none help her,' he said.

'And the lamb?' said Francis. But Francis was standing at a safe distance, by the sled.

'The lamb may be dead already. I will roll up thy sleeve,' said Thomas. Then he knelt at the ewe's head, and spoke soft words to it.

'I can't,' I said.

'It is but one of God's creatures, as we are,' said Thomas. 'Like us of blood and bone and slime. Take pity, wench, for you are of her kind.'

Then I knelt down in the snow, and taking the lamb's hooves in my left hand I thrust them in again.

'Now,' said Thomas, 'the head will be free. Reach in and feel for it, and press it down. Canst thou feel it?'

My hand slipped on slimy hardness in the loathsome warmth of the ewe's bowels. 'I think so,' I said. 'I think I feel an ear.'

'Press the head hard down,' said Thomas, 'and pull upon the hooves. Pull with what might thou hast, little maid!'

The lamb came smooth and sudden. It gushed onto the snow and lay there, steaming. I was blood to my elbow, and blood lay upon the snow. But the foul little creature bleated faintly where it lay, and my heart lifted at the sound in purest joy and made me smile at Thomas from my heart.

'What is thy name?' he asked me.

17

'Mall Percival.'

'And how old art thou, Mall?' he asked me, smiling back.

'I am eight summers,' I told him, watching while the ewe struggled round to find and lick her lamb.

'Thou hast a good stout stomach for one so young,' he said. 'Hold still while I clean thee.' He took a bunch of snow in his huge hands, and rubbed it down my arms and hands till I burned with the cold, and came clean again. And Francis standing by.

Thomas pulled the sled back to where the others had been, but they had departed home. So he trudged on, pulling me and Francis right to the townhead of Eyam, and there he took leave of us.

'I am glad the lamb lived,' I said, taking the rope of the sled from him.

'The loss of the ewe would have been a graver matter,' he said, and left us at once, to stride away back to the uplands.

My sled had scarcely been used since. There was a deal of rust to scrape down if the new parson's son was to have the loan of it, come the snow, in the year in which I and Francis were sixteen.

There had not yet been a Sunday since the new parson came, when Thomas Heald was trapped down a narrow vein in the Glebe Mine. He was one of only three copers digging there, and they had worked the vein down to water, trying to get out the ore they had bargained for to get. When he fell into the water, the other two could not pull him out. There was hue and cry up and down the street, both ways from the Bull Ring in the midst of town, for the mine opened just beside the street there, in a little arch propped up with wood. Someone came running for Mary Gregory, whose father was one of the two copers down there, trying to draw Thomas out of the water, and Mary was sitting in Catherine Momphesson's house, busy with sewing a seam into a curtain that was making for the parson's bed. Mary jumped up and ran out at once, going down the street from the parsonage as fast as she could, and Catherine Momphesson jumped up too and went with her, running at her heels, and came into the crowd that was thronging there.

'I fear his legs be caught beneath the water,' John Gregory was saying. 'For we cannot lift him. The place is so narrow we can heave but one at a time. And but we lift him soon the cold will dull him, and he will be lost.'

'I will go down and get him,' cried Marshall Howe, in his loud, roaring voice.

'Rather let me try,' said Robert Wood.

'Try a fall with me, and we'll soon see who's the stronger!' cried Marshall Howe.

And at that, 'Peace, neighbours,' said Thomas Stanley, the old parson, who had no need to raise his voice to have a hearing. 'Go both and try, and God grant you contrive it.'

Marshall Howe and Robert Wood were certainly the biggest and strongest men in Eyam, and little like to do anything together in an ordinary case, for Marshall was a foulmouthed, cursing sort of man, often deep in drink, and barely able to give a wench good morning without giving offence, and Robert Wood was a Quaker of a most sober and quiet demeanour, who neither drank nor sang, nor gave good morning to any, but was the most silent man in Eyam. They two now went together, crawling into the mine-head, leaving the throng waiting, and poor Mary Heald in mortal fear among them with her children, and wringing of her hands.

Thomas Stanley began a prayer, but was soon cut short. John Gregory came up again, saying the rope they had around poor Thomas Heald was but thin twine and was cutting his flesh as fast as they drew him up by it. He called for something softer, but strong and of a good length; and voices rose again, asking who had a bolt of cloth, or a rope of good thickness handy. And while some goodwives were pulling off their petticoats right in the very street, and knotting them together, somehow the parson's new bed-curtain was handed forward, torn in two and knotted once, and that went down the mine as soon as John Gregory spied it.

So Thomas Heald was brought up to the daylight, more dead than alive it seemed, and laid out on the verge at the roadside. They cut the flowering turf from the green wayside, and laid his face next the naked earth, while Thomas Stanley said it were better to have him in haste next a fire to warm his blood, than to follow such foolish superstition. By and by he was carried home, and laid in his own bed, reviving.

There were many offering to help Mistress Heald; and she first asked that someone would find her children, for they had been with her but now in the crowd at the mine door, and were now not to be found, and she had no time to seek after them. They were quickly found, sitting in the Rectory kitchen, playing a game of knuckle-bones with Catherine herself, and eating little comfits from her pantry.

'I thought better they saw not their father brought forth, before their eyes, lest he had been . . . but, God be thanked, you may have them home again now!' she said, and sent them off with their pockets full of comfits, and smiling.

Mary Gregory with a long face brought in the fouled and dripping curtains to the kitchen, fearing her mistress's wrath – for she had newly become the maidservant in the Rectory. But Catherine Momphesson said, 'I am right glad I bought a goodly calico, and not a silk at far more expense; for this will wash, Mary, and we will have it right again. Alas, the seam you spent the morning on is rent apart, and must be done again!'

'But it was impudence to run in here, and take such goods as these for such a purpose,' said Mary. 'Whoever can have done it?'

'I did,' said Catherine.

*

20

When Sunday came all the Eyam people were in their pews, even Thomas Stanley, right at the back. The new parson spoke soft, and told us he would not force the changes on us all at once. We heard the hated service from the Old Prayer Book, new restored, with stony faces and hard hearts. We heard him say he would not deck the altar yet as in a heathen temple, nor watch to see who bowed not at the name of Jesus. 'You will find me gentle, that you may get used to change by slow degrees,' he said.

'Are there degrees of idolatry?' murmured John Stanley at the back, but his father clapped a hand upon his mouth.

We got no sermon that Sunday. The service was done full two hours sooner than we looked for, and we sent forth with no good teaching to sustain us.

Little good the parson got of his gentleness. 'He is not serious,' Rachel Trickett said. 'If he believed this churchery with as fixed a mind as we have to our faith, he would not speak of taking time, but would tell us strongly what he trusts is right.' And she, and we, were among many folk who after the service sat down in the garden behind Thomas Stanley's house, and heard the Bible read, passing it round who could read.

There were few in Eyam who thought well of the new parson. But a pretty face, and a pinch of good sense and good will, and a pair of calico bedcurtains had brought it about already that his Catherine was beyond reproach among us.

There was sledding enough for Master Momphesson in the winter that next followed. The snow came in the last days of October and lasted till March, with a thaw at Christmas that was frozen over again by Twelfth Night. The springs froze, and the basin called the river needed breaking every morning that we might draw water, and sometimes must be broken again at mid-day. The parson's son soon better liked to keep himself by the fire than to come forth into the snow to play. All the children grew weary of sledding, and there was still more snow. So that when tardily the spring came in it was full welcome to us all. The snowdrop and aconite stood close above the leaf-mould on the woodland floors, and the grass broke green, and it was good and pleasant to go up to the sheepruns, instead of bitter and full of hardship.

I well remember the day when Emmot Sydall came out to me as I passed by her door early, and said, 'Mall, if thou goest walking on the uplands this fine morn, I have a mind to go with thee.'

'Nay, Emmot,' I said. 'I go but to see after my sheep how they are faring, and give them care.'

'Then I will go to thy sheep likewise, and see the pretty lambs,' she said.

I saw it was no use to deny her, for I could not keep her from following me, whatever I said to her; but she looked at me very slyly as she spoke, so that my heart was heavy and I feared she knew my secrets. Emmot was a wayward girl, the prettiest young woman of Eyam, and very headstrong; I would not have had her among dozens to be my trust-friend.

But we passed up the town street together, from her house opposite the churchyard gate, beside the Inn. By the river, running now cool and fresh with sweet melt-water, we passed some children playing, jumping in a swinging rope, and chanting,

> 'Baslow for gentlefolk,
> Calver for Trenchers,
> Middleton for rogues and thieves,
> And Eyam for pretty wenches!'

I saw Emmot blush many shades at this. And I thought, though I spoke not my thought, 'Ah, Emmot, in Parson Stanley's days thou wouldst not have dared know thyself a pretty wench, for fear of a damnation upon vanity!' And I smiled to myself.

The piping song rang behind us as we went on,

'Ashford in the water,
Longstone in the lice,
Sheldon in the nutwood,
And Bakewell in the spice!...'

We came in a few steps to the fork in the road where straight on led upon our way, and to the right lay the approach to the new hall that was building for the Bradshaws.

'Let us take a step to see how the hall goes, Mall,' said Emmot. And since we had set out together, whether I would or no, I went with her. We stood and gazed upon the hall; a fine fair building, of clean-cut new stone, three storeys high and with great windows that would need a deal of glass to close them in. The masons were working to the eaves upon planks and ladders and before the pleasant door the carpenters were making ready the roof-timbers to go up.

'There will be nothing to compare with this fair house,' said Emmot, 'for many miles around.'

'Indeed not,' said a girl's voice from behind us. 'But it is time we had a dwelling worthy our station.'

We found the Squire's lady and his daughter had come upon us as we stood and stared. Fine ladies both, all in finespun, and good Nottingham lace. The daughter had been reared and schooled in Derby, and though we had seen her often enough, neither she nor her mother spoke often to us. 'It will be so fine,' the daughter now said to us, 'you cannot imagine. And all furnished with comforts and fair appurtenances. The hangings for the solar are even now come up from Mortlake. Would you like to see them?'

I hung back, but Emmot answered yes, and eagerly. So we were led in to a fine barn, finished to the roof, that lay a little to one side of the house, and there was a great stack of hay on one side the door, and goods and furnishings all piled up on the other.

'Father would have the barn made first!' said his daughter.

'There had to be fodder for the horses to cart the stone,' said Mistress Bradshaw, and showing us three great boxes standing by, braced with iron corners, she lifted the lid of one, and turned back the wrap of hessian within, that we might see a corner of the folded tapestry stored away therein. We saw a fair flowered border, and then a part of a picture, all worked in the finest coloured wools, in a manner of working and weaving I had never seen before, and marvellously skilled. We could see but a foot, clad in a boot of blue leather, and with a feathered wing upon the heel, stepping on a turf of flowered grass.

'What is it?' I asked.

'It is Hermes, bringing news,' answered the young Mistress.

'What book is that in?' I asked next, meaning of the Bible, which book.

'Oh, some tale of the Greek gods,' the girl answered.

'A *heathen* book?' I was amazed.

'Daughter, what use is it to vaunt ourselves before such village maids as these!' said Mistress Bradshaw, scornfully.

'I think it is of wondrous workmanship,' said Emmot, stretching out a hand to finger the border, gingerly. 'Look, Mall, is it not so?'

But at her touch the Bradshaws frowned, and the young Mistress twitched the wrapping back over, and closed the box lid.

'I should like to see all the picture, when I may,' said Emmot, boldly.

'Perhaps when it is all hung upon the walls you may come in and see it, Emmot Sydall,' said the elder, relenting. Emmot thanked her for this promise. I said nothing, for it

24

had not been made to me; and we left them and went on our way.

'So it is only to tend your flock that you go out, rain or shine?' said Emmot in a while, as we came to the top of the slope in the road, and had the rolling upland all before us.

'Yes.'

'And not to meet with any?'

'Why ask me that?' I said. 'Does not all the world well know that a flock of sheep needs tending?' But anxiously I wondered what she knew, and how.

'Well, but you are not a poor man's daughter, that you need to keep sheep. How comes it that Mall is a shepherdess at all?' She was half laughing; teasing, brimming over with something.

'Oh, Emmot,' said I, 'you know how it was. You were there on the day Thomas found me to bring the lamb forth in the snow. And because I had saved it, after Thomas gave it me.'

He had brought it to the house across his shoulders, grown on a bit, but still very small. And clearly I yet remembered how he stood upon the threshhold, and told my mother that the lamb was mine.

My father had frowned. 'We have no need of it,' he had said. 'My daughter need not busy herself with the beasts of the field and fell. I keep her in apparel and in meat, and she can sit in warmth and ease, and ply the needle like a lady born. Well, well, we thank thee, but we have no need. Take thou the lamb again.'

My mother looked sharply at my face, and said to me in a low voice, 'Dost thou want the lamb, Mall?'

I nodded, with my eyes smarting with tears, and not trusting myself to speak.

'Fie, husband!' cried my mother. 'What art thou thinking of? Turning a good mutton dinner from the door, and a fleece of wool upon its back that will stuff a good bolster? Now God be thanked we are not in need, through thy hard

25

work and careful managing, but shall we therefore be thrift-less? Let the child have the lamb, and get herself good by it.'

'This goodman is not kin of ours, nor friend, nor even from our parish,' said my father. 'Shall we take gifts from strangers, wife, as though we were beggars?'

'I am Thomas Torre, cousin to Torres in Eyam, and Torres in Middleton,' the lad said, 'and right ready to be friend of thine, as of any man. And the lamb I owe to thy daughter, for that she saved the ewe for me, without which it would not have lived to have brought forth this second lamb. And the gift will be nothing worth but the little maid will coddle it, and feed it with milk upon her fingers; the ewe cannot sustain it.'

'Oh, father . . .' I said.

'Ah, be it so then,' said Father, giving way to our will. 'But, wife, the neighbours will all be saying I have lost the money I lay out in maintaining mines, and we are brought so low that our daughter must keep sheep!'

'Fie, husband!' said my mother again. 'Did not the Lord himself call himself a shepherd? And where in the Bible does it talk of maintainers of mines?'

'Give over, woman,' my father said. 'Did I not say yes, and doth that not suffice for thee? Go get a cup of milk and an oaten cake to give this Thomas for his pains.'

So Thomas put the lamb into my arms, and promised to instruct me in its care. All that long since; the day Emmot came out with me I had twelve ewes, and a ram, and nine lambs come or coming that spring, from natural increase, and a strong young dog that Thomas bought me at Tides-well market, when at shearing time we sold my clip, and trained to pliancy for me. He was called Ranter, for the barking and growling he made about his work; and as I walked with Emmot he was running as ever at my heels.

'A bird told me,' Emmot said, 'thou goest every day to meet with Thomas, rather than thy sheep.'

'Alas what mischief is this, Emmot?' I said. 'My sheep

26

run with Thomas's sheep. Thus when I work, I see him like as not.'

'But, ah, the bird sang me a different song, Mall, and told me that he calls you Mouse, and dreams of you the day-long, and not displeases you. And the bird told me further, that Thomas would speak to your father, but that you and your mother fear he would be sent off at once, for that your father is become a greater and a greater man these last few years and looks not to have his child wed a common shepherd. And so you keep silence, that at least none will stop you from keeping sheep, and meeting with him . . . Is it not so, Mall?'

'Oh, Emmot!' I cried. 'It is not so!'

'I think it is,' she said.

'It is in your power, Emmot, to do us both much harm. If this should get about, the gossips of the town . . .'

'I will not speak of it, Mall,' she said. 'I would not harm you for anything. Why should I so? Did you not share your spice pies with me, the day your father brought you some from Bakewell?' Still she was laughing, as she spoke.

'Thou art not known for keeping secrets, Emmot,' said I bitterly. 'And where canst thou have learned this one? Is it already noised about the town?'

'Mall, trust me for it, for I have changed, I swear,' she said, suddenly very grave and quiet. 'I learned about you from your Thomas's cousin, Roland Torre of Middleton. It was your Thomas himself who told Roland; they are close cousins, and have been friends from babes.'

'Why, then, how ill did this Roland do, to take his cousin's secret, and tell it abroad!' I said, and vexation and dread brought tears into my eyes.

'But I am not "abroad" that he told it,' she said, gently. 'He and I are sweethearts, Mall, and are to be wed in good time.' She turned on me a shining face, and said, 'I am so happy, Mall, that when I go to walk my footsteps dance beneath my skirts! Wish me well, Mall. I am to be handfasted at the Wakes; my father gives a feast then for all our kinsfolk who will come from miles around.'

'In good truth, I wish you well,' I said. I was confused at Emmot so changed, and so quickly going from laughter to gravity and back again.

'I know I have not been a friend to thee, in special, Mall, and not always kind,' she said, blushing a little, 'but if thou wilt let me, I will be thy good friend now. My Roland has asked me about you; when we are man and wife his father will give him a good independence, and he will make shift to help you and Thomas if he can.'

By this time we had arrived within view of the flocks, and there was Thomas, leaning upon his staff, with his two dogs, waiting for me.

'Who have you brought, Mouse?' he asked.

'Emmot Sydall,' said I.

'Why, and I took my cousin for a great moonstruck romancer, and all for telling me true!' said Thomas, smiling at her.

'A fine family, the Torres!' she said jauntily in return. 'Mall, which of all these sheep are thine?'

So then we whistled to the dogs. They sped like arrows round the scattered, grazing sheep, and he whistled and cried, 'Away, away, away, away, away! By, by, by!' and they divided mine from the rest, and brought them, bleating, to us.

We showed her what we were about, assuring ourselves that the new lambs were not sickly and were sucking well, making good guess in our wisdom which ewes would next and soonest drop their lambs . . . but having said her say, she soon lost all her care to see the sheep, and wandered off singing to herself, and picking primroses on the brim of a tiny stream.

'Why are you sad, Mouse?' Thomas asked me.

'It touches on our safety, love. She hath an idle, clacking tongue, and an edge of spite . . .'

'Nay, love,' he said. 'Doth not love make lovers all con-spire against the whole world else? Do you not smile to see her in this plight?'

I did smile. And on the homeward path, as we again passed by the children, still with their rope at play, I did her better justice in my mind. Sure, it was not at 'Eyam for pretty wenches' she had blushed so deep, but at 'Middleton for rogues and thieves'. Her Roland's father was the biggest man in Middleton.

Emmot's handfasting to young Roland was soon known abroad, and giving a feast of cheerful gossip up and down the town. And Emmot was as good as her word, and had become kind and gentle to me. She brought me a pottle of strawberries from her mother's garden when they were ripe, and came to talk to me of how her parlour should be furnished, and suchlike. She learned soon that I was cun-ning with my needle, and sweetly asked my help and company when her store of linens was in the making. I spun some of my own fleeces for her, and helped her willingly enough, though I never lost a care of what words I spoke when I was with her, knowing her from of old.

The time I spent with Emmot would have been longer had not the season of summer that year – the year of Our Lord 1665 – been of prodigious drought. The oldest men amongst us could not remember any like it. For nigh on three months we were without any mercy of rain. A glaring haze masked the sun, and the sky looked like dully bur-nished metal. What clouds we saw had no edges, but looked like bruises on the heavens. Our fluent streams dried up – the small ones vanished utterly, leaving the track of pell-mell stones dusty and silent; the larger waters broke apart into still and separate pools, with sluggish waters of oily smoothness, and dusty surfaces with specks of blown earth and fallen seeds. There came to be almost no green, in all Eyam's wide prospects, for the leaves on the trees darkened almost to grey, or withered to early brown; the burnt grass lay golden far and wide, but for a bright fringe at the margins of any water remaining; and trees in high places began to die as the water sank away from their roots. It was a desolation as of March, and the hues of March, all in July, and into August. And it gave shepherd folk work to do, for our poor beasts could not forage for themselves in such a time.

It was three nights before the Wakes, and I came home by moonlight from a long evening bringing my sheep to water and to some fresher grass, far off by a diminished spring, and bringing them back again. Francis Archdale was with me, my father having asked him neighbourly to come for me, that I might not be alone in the nightfall. We two were ambushed by Bridget Teylor and Eliza Abel, who came to us creeping from their gates, and speaking low.

'Mall, thou canst write, canst thou not?' said Bridget.

'That I can.'

'Wilt thou help Eliza, Mall? We have need of thee.'

'I can write,' said Francis.

'This is a woman's matter,' said Eliza. 'Stand away a step, Francis, that thou hear us not.'

'This it is, Mall,' said Bridget. 'Eliza was hoping for Roland Torre, whom Emmot Sydall is to have. Her father had set her on to hope for him, and they had met and gone walking in the Cussy Dell together; and now he is to be another's. And Eliza cannot rid herself of tenderness and grief for him. Poor wench, she cannot sleep the night.'

And indeed, as Bridget spoke the moonlight showed a shining tear-track on Eliza's face.

'But how can I help this?' I asked them. 'How could any help it?'

'We went to Goody Trickett for a charm,' said Bridget, 'for they say she can charm and heal ailments of every kind. And she told us to write Eliza's affliction upon a paper, and set it at a safe distance, and it would take off whatever grief

30

was written on it. But for herself, she cannot write. We asked Mistress Momphesson, but she scolded us, saying it was an idle trick, and for shame, we should go pray; and we asked John Stanley, and he said it was devil's work, and then I bethought me that thou canst write. Eliza was afraid to ask you, for that you have become Emmot's friend of late, but I said you were not a one to put new friends in front of old. Nor can it do Emmot any hurt, Mall, though it may do Eliza good.'

'It was not for such folly that I learned to write,' I said. But then Eliza choked a little on her tears, and I thought what plight I would be in were Thomas handfasted to another, and so I took pity on her.

To Francis I said, 'I pray thee, Francis, go tell my father I am within the town, and will be home presently,' and I stepped into Bridget's house. Her parents were abed in a chamber above, and the fire burned low in the hearth. Bridget lit a candle for us, by which I well saw how woebegone Eliza looked.

'What shall I write?' I asked, Bridget bringing me a paper and a charred twig from the fire.

'Goody Trickett said, write what we would be rid of, and put the paper away.'

So I wrote, '*That love and liking for Roland Torre, which is in the heart of Elizabeth Abel, and those images of him which do possess her, together with dreams, hopes, yearns, and sundry imaginations . . .*' And this I read over to them.

Then Eliza snatched up the paper and cast it into the fire, and we three watched the brief blaze of it on the embers. And Eliza gave me a posy of ribbons for my pains, and kissed me, saying we might all wear ribbons at the Wakes, now Parson Stanley was set aside. And I went home, hoping my father would not ask on what matter I had been kept, for it was not for making charms that he had taught me my letters but that I might read the Bible; just as he had taught me to cipher so that I might keep the reckoning

31

books of his contracts in the mines after his time, he having no son.

That same hot blazing weather that made hardship for my hapless sheep promised well for the Wakes. There had been never so many folk gathered to them before; not a family but had their kin on the road coming to them. There was to be an ox roasted whole, and dances – a morris, to be sure, but boy with girl also, and a group of folk living in the Lydgate were dressing their well-head with a flower picture of Robin Goodfellow, though that tale be not in the Bible. Richard Sydall and his wife Elizabeth held a great feast for Emmot's handfasting. Sydalls from far and wide were bidden to it, and Torres almost as many from parishes far and near, and Richard Sydall laid out lavishly in food and drink for all. He invited the new parson, but not the old – thus setting tongues to wag – and strangely, he invited my father, my mother and me. It took my mother but three minutes' thought to hit on the reason that my father could not guess at all; my mother knew who was kin to whom for miles and miles around. I feared my father would not accept to go.

'I much mislike, wife,' he said, 'being singled out in this way above other honest households. None in the town but have known Richard Sydall since a child – why does he ask us, and not, forsooth, the Archdales?'

'He could not ask all, husband. He needs must choose.'

'I am not any bosom friend of his.'

'He is a good honest neighbour, William, whom it would be folly to offend.'

'Offend him? We will not offend him. I purpose we will go. Only I would go with a lighter heart if I could figure why.'

I looked up then from my sewing, as though I would have spoken, and saw my mother, standing close behind my father's chair, lay her finger upon her lips at me.

'Our Mall has been helping Emmot with her dower linen,' she said. 'She has been often there, wearing her thimble thin.' She spoke as though the thought had just struck her.

'Ah,' said my father. 'Well, perhaps that's it, wife.'

'It must be that,' my mother said.

The Wakes had never gone so well, as long as any could remember. Every maid in ribbons, and ribbons in the young men's hats; every face full of smiles for some friend or kinsman come; the sun shining welcome all the long day; the little children running about giving posies of meadow-weeds and daisies, gathered at daybreak, and getting blessings and comfits and apples back again. The new parson's two children joined in this playing with a will, and ran about so much they were found at last forwearied, fast asleep curled up together on the grass by the baker's stall, and were taken up sleeping and carried home again.

One thing only befell to mar the day. Young Will, rough Marshall Howe's yet rougher son, and some of his cronies being aswill with strong ale by noon that day, fell to mocking and cursing the new parson's Old Prayer Book, and in their stupor they drove into the church a cow new calved, and chased the dumb creature round about the font, and as they did this chanting, *'Forasmuch as it hath pleased God to give you safe deliverance, and hath preserved you in great danger of childbirth, you shall therefore give hearty thanks unto God and say: Moo! moo! moo!'* Thus in their riot they made mock of the service for the Churching of Women, and the poor tormented cow, missing her calf, bellowed loudly, and blundered about, and soiled the floor.

Mistress Cooper heard the uproar, and brought the churchwardens, and a bucket to clean up the filth.

'What will you do, then?' yelled Will Howe. 'Will ye tell 't to the parson?' and he laughed.

But the wardens, taking their belts to the business, dealt

33

out thrashing instead, and finished up with a threat that should the new parson learn of it, the old would be brought in to chide them all; and then the great silly youths, being too drunk to fend off blows, ran away chastened to sleep off their bellyfuls.

And so much was afoot in Eyam that day, and so great the sounds of mirth and joy, that only a few folk would ever have known about the churching of the cow had not Mistress Cooper's ready tongue made a tale of it to one and all, upon the morrow. It blunted not our joy upon the day. The laughing and dancing went on longer than the long summer light, and lasted under the stars in the sweet cool of evening. I danced much with Thomas, and a little with Francis and Abel and Dan to cover my tracks, and once with Roland Torre, who fetched me for his partner, and as he turned me about and about at the top of the figure, murmured to me that Thomas was a good fellow . . .

When the dusk began to gather Thomas danced me right off the end of the row, and away under the trees in his arms. 'Mall . . .' he said soft to me, 'Mall . . .' Then we heard a dry cough, and looking startled round we saw that Parson Stanley was standing at the edge of the trees, looking at the dancing and festival, while lanterns were lit here, there and everywhere, and he on the margins of the dark. He had a sad countenance. I thought he had not been watching us, but all the rest, but Thomas said quickly, 'Mall will not come to any harm with me, Parson.'

'What?' he said, turning his gaze full on us. 'No, indeed.' I thought he would say no more, he stood so long silent, and we stood uneasy, liking not to turn back to the revel, nor yet to stand our ground.

Then he said, 'Young Thomas Torre, sirrah, thou hast by the hand the only maid in Eyam that can read a book. Have her teach thee thy letters.'

'What need of that have I?' said Thomas in astoundment, 'I but a shepherd . . .'

'There is no preaching now,' the parson said, speaking sad and low. 'Or all but none. And what there is . . . see already how the people forsake virtue. 'Tis small things now; only ribbands and posies . . . but anon . . . and for any that can read, the word of God is at hand, and none can keep them from it. In the time coming we shall sorely need that word.'

'I have no Bible, sir,' said Thomas. His voice was troubled.

'I will give thee one, that day thou comest to me, able to read a page.'

'What page will you have him read?' I said.

'Matthew five,' he told me, 'wherein you both may read: *"Blessed are the pure in heart, for they shall see God."*'

'Well,' said Thomas. 'Well. Come, Mall.' And drawing me by the hand he ran me back to join the dancers in the bright lantern-light, and the squeal of the scraping fiddle, leaving Parson Stanley where he stood.

And as Thomas whirled me round, I saw that our other, our new Parson Momphesson was in the dance himself, dandling his pretty wife upon his arm, and stepping lightly, with a smile on his wide face from ear to ear, and I stood stock still a moment and missed my step, thinking of that other parson, all alone in the leafy darkness, looking on.

Though Catherine Momphesson looked lovely enough, dancing and laughing in the lantern-light in the Wakes of Eyam, it was in her old gown that she looked so; for the pattern for her new dress was not yet come. The tailor had kept busy making other girls' garments. The marvellous fine weather saw out the Wakes and lasted a few days longer; then in September in a run of great thunderstorms it broke, and rained long and heavily. At once it seemed the grass sprang new again, and the burned plains of scorched yellow were broken with a tender haze of blades of such brilliant green as we never before had seen. A week after the rain the whole land blazed emerald under the trees too early bronzed. The sheep ate bellyfuls at last, and gave us better hope they might gain strength enough against the winter dearth, of which we had given up hoping for.

And the tailor's parcel came up at last from London, set down on Widow Cooper's doorstep with George Vicars's name written clear and large upon it, and was found to be drenched with damp.

The tailor exclaimed in annoyance over the parcel. He tutted and clucked so loudly that Mistress Cooper stepped through from her kitchen to ask what ailed, and he prayed her for a knife to cut through the twine round the sodden bale of goods. 'He would not set his scissors to the twine, though they were even in his hand at that moment,' said Mistress Cooper, telling the tale to my mother. A knife being brought him, Goodman Vicars undid his patterns. They were a set of fancy shapes in sackcloth, or coarse canvas, and the rain had got into the parcel and wet it right through. The tailor put a line across the room, and hung up the patterns before the fire to dry. The rain pelted the little window panes from without, and soon they sweated and ran within from the mist of the drying cloth. Steam wisps rose faintly off the canvas, and Mistress Cooper went back to her breadmaking, leaving the tailor sitting on the floor, staring at his drying-line, putting the pieces together, as she supposed, in his mind, figuring out how the outlandish dress was to be made.

He sat on till supper-time, and later, sewing – Mistress Cooper thought but languidly – at a collar that he had to finish, and staring at the homespun patterns. When Mistress Cooper lit her candle to go up to bed he still sat, fingering his needle. She offered him a ladle of milk, and he would not have it, but only water. Everything in the room was moist, everything sweating with the steamy air from the drying out of the cloth, and there was a stale and dirty smell given off by the stuff. Even the tailor's brow was beaded with damp, and he sat so still that there was not stir enough in the room to fright the rats from creeping about the floor. They fled away at Mistress Cooper's heavy tread, bringing the water. She counselled him to sleep presently, and he thanked her for her care. It seemed to her that the stench from the parcel had filled up all the house, so she threw open the casement in the room where she and her sons slept, and the sound of the rain outside kept her long wakeful. She did not hear the tailor come up the stairs to his garret.

When she arose in the morning, Mistress Cooper found the fire burning merrily, so that it was clear it had been but lately mended, and the patterns were all bone dry and folded neatly, lying in a pile upon the tailor's chest in the window-corner. The drying-line was coiled upon its hook, and the room all set to rights, so that she thought nothing amiss and went about her errands. The tailor did not rise up and set to work at his usual time, but she thought he was oversleeping the late hour of the last evening. And she was bound to Bakewell that day, taking her sons with her, for she was seeking an apprenticeship for Edward, he being now about fourteen, and he had an uncle in Bakewell, a saddler, who might set him on.

It was five o'clock when they came back from Bakewell, and she was now much struck that the tailor was not sitting in his usual place, plying his needle. So going up to the loft below the eaves where he slept, she found him lying very sick, and parched for water. As night came on his fever worsened, and taking pity on him, though he was not kin of hers, Mistress Cooper called upon Goody Trickett, who came and left a pinch of herbs to make a tea to give him to drink.

Though it had cost her a groat it did little good, for on the morrow the poor goodman was worse. A hideous huge swelling had grown up upon his neck, that pushed his head

37

crooked on his pallet, and grievously pained him. His words were wild and he knew not where he was, nor could he remember Mistress Cooper's name, but wildly gave some wench's name from long ago.

Hearing that he was sick, Mistress Momphesson came to visit him, and climbed the narrow steps to his room, and when he saw her his senses returned a moment, for he said, 'Alas, my girl, your London dress...'

'Be of good courage, Master Vicars,' said she. 'I shall wear it yet!'

'No! No!' cried he, starting up, and falling again upon the bed.

'I will fetch forth my husband to pray with thee,' she said; and once she was gone he howled for Mistress Cooper, and implored her to burn the patterns. His words were furious as he tore at the bedding with frantic hands; and she could make not head nor tail of the half of what he said so wildly, but she understood clear enough that she should burn the patterns, and that in haste. They could not with safety be put upon the hearth, so she took them into the garden, and her two sons set fire to them with a hot coal and stood over the smoking pile till all was consumed to ashes; the sick man would have no peace till she could tell him it was done.

Parson Momphesson came in the evening, but the tailor would not hear him, and swore and blasphemed fearfully. The parson said calmly that it was but the fever speaking and not the man's soul. He gave a blessing, and spoke a prayer from the bed-foot, and was gone. The tailor howled and moaned piteously for half the night, and then was quiet. When Parson Stanley came to visit him, secretly, at first light, he was found dead.

All this I know because it was much on Mistress Cooper's mind, both then and later, and she told it all over both in the gross and in the detail to any that would hear her patiently; and my poor mother was one of those who would. I have sat spinning, and heard it all told time and again, to the dew on the windows, and on the tailor's brow.

It was a sorry tale, and we had some grief of it. Many Eyam folk brought the late flowers from their garths to cover the bare earth of the grave. The church was full, and there were many to follow the corpse to the grave in the far churchyard corner, to join in prayer for him. But he had been a stranger in the village, and had not dwelt long among us. All but Mistress Cooper put him very soon out of mind. What special cause for fear she might have had she did not speak of to any at that time.

It was the sixth of September, the year of Our Lord 1665, that George Vicars died. He was buried on the seventh. Buried, and forgotten for a fortnight.

Right well do I remember the season when George Vicars was buried. The weather was soft and sweet; the hills still held the warmth of the long summer's heat, but the rainfall had cleansed and sweetened the land. The streams all ran again, and there was good drinking for men and sheep, and the new grass was springing everywhere in so marvellous a bright green our common hills might have been lawns in paradise. Yet though the grass looked spring-like, the golden blaze of autumn had come early upon the trees, and in Eyam none remembered any September like it, for a fair season.

That time I was meeting Thomas with the flocks each and every day; and as soon as our tending was done we would find a quiet spot and sit down together, and I would bring out my slate from my apron pocket and set to teach him his letters, with a stub of chalk, and our two heads leaning down together over the little slate. There was a way to sit very close, side by side, and even for me to take his hand in mine, and push it round a making of 'O' or 'M' and no harm thought of. I taught him 'Thomas' and I taught him 'Blessed are the Meek' and I taught him 'I am the Good

Shepherd', and he learned these, teasing me all the while with asking to be shown 'Mouse' and 'Mall' and 'I love thee, my sweetheart'.

'Fie, Thomas,' I rebuked him, 'what will Parson Stanley say if he find thou canst write nought but "I love thee, sweet Mouse"?'

'It is not for Parson Stanley that I bend my wits to this, Mall,' he said, smiling, 'but for thee.'

'Tush, tush,' I said.

'But soberly, though,' he said, one of his moments of gravity coming suddenly upon his face. 'For writing, I have little mind; but I can see that a man would do well to read. Forget the slate, Mouse, and bring to me a book, and I will be thy most diligent apprentice!'

And so full early one morning, on a day brilliant with dew in the bright sunrise, I walked down the street and to the door of the Coopers' cottage. Young Edward opened the door to me, with a cup of milk in his hand, and his collar unfastened, and he blushed a little to see me, which made me to fix my face very sad for fear of laughing at him, for he was a good lad, and though he did trail after me and make occasion to speak to me, I was not minded to mock him. My mother said while the great lads mooned after maids older in years than they, there was no need to worry; it was when they went after the younger ones it was time they should be close watched!

I would not step in, but stood on the doorstep in the sun; and when Edward brought his mother to me I asked her that I might borrow the little Bible, printed small, that had been in the tailor's box and of which she had spoken. I undertook she should have it again by nightfall. My father's Bible was as big as a flagstone step, and half as heavy. Saying, 'Have a care of it, Mall, for it is not mine,' she lent it me, and I went on my way. Edward came with me a step or two, smiling, and promising to bring me cakes and comfits when he came home from Bakewell next.

At the head of the town I took leave of him and went running upon my way, burning with eagerness to be with Thomas on the hills. I would hitch up my heavy skirts with my shepherd's crook, and free my feet for running and leaping across rocky ground. So I came up to Thomas, as always, out of breath.

We sat by a little fresh running spring, under a wind-stunted hawthorn all bright with haws, while the sheep bleated round us and the bell-wether ding-donged. First we bent our minds upon the Bible, and letter by letter we spelt out the tally of blesseds: blessed are the poor in spirit, and they that mourn, and the meek, and they which do hunger and thirst after righteousness . . . and then Thomas played an air upon his pipe.

When the sun was high overhead and the patch of shade we sat in was shrunk to a kerchief size, we heard voices near by. I was ill pleased at any company, but Thomas stood up and hailed them, and there were Emmot and her Roland, he with a basket on his arm, come to seek us. They had brought bread and cheese and a jar of ale, and we all sat down together and ate heartily. Roland held Emmot by the hand, which made Thomas bold to take mine also. Emmot looked at Roland sideways with such a shine upon her face as made me smile to see. Roland Torre was but a man; of medium stature, plain features and dark hair. She looked upon him as if he had been a London gallant, or at least an angel; but he was not handsome, except when he looked at her.

When we had eaten Thomas piped and Roland and Emmot danced. Then as we set down again together Thomas had a tale to tell. He said as he came across the sheep-walks that morning, he had met a stranger upon the road – a fat man in a dusty cloak, covered with twigs and burrs as if he had slept in a bush – who asked him for a draught of water from his flagon. Thomas had given of it gladly enough, and the stranger then set forth a bushel of

41

talking, all dark and hard to Thomas, but of which he understood this much, that the stranger bade him seek to see the world by inner light, which should shine very bright and clear, and show him all he would ever need to know or see.

'What answer didst thou make, cousin?' Roland asked.

'Why, I told him a shepherd on the hills had always light enough to see by,' Thomas said. 'How even in the storm when the great clouds roll above, the sun puts fingers through, and how when the sky is clear our hills are lit as though they were at the gates of paradise. And shortly, that I looked to see well enough by God's own daylight!'

'What answered he again?' asked Roland.

'He told me that a man must have inner light to see the outer by, and a good deal more Sunday talk. So I told him cheerily today was Thursday, and took my road!'

Roland laughed and challenged Thomas to race him to the ridge, which race Thomas won easily, while Emmot and I looked on. Then he and she parted from Thomas and me, and we sat a while alone, with little said but much contentment in our quiet. In a while Thomas said, 'I mean to have you, Mall. I would rather die, else. When may I ask thy father?'

'Patience, Thomas, love,' I said. 'Thou shalt have me, anon.'

'What if he marry you to some richer man?' said Thomas, turning his head away.

'He does not think of it, yet. And he would find he could not; I would not consent. My mother is our friend in this, love. She will see all well in time.'

'I would not tarry much longer, love,' he said.

I went home in a purple dusk, pricked out in stars, like a meadow in buttercups. The streamlets murmured, and the birds of evening sang. A scatter of windows, of candlelight, or lantern-light, like a broken string of golden beads, showed me my town below me. I stepped down past half

42

the houses to my own door. As on my deathbed, in my mind I shall walk home that evening, I shall never forget the walking, and the coming to my door, for that it was the last time ever I was light of heart, or of good hope and courage, or safe in my own place. I stood a moment with my hand upon the latch, thinking of Thomas and smiling in the darkness, and then went in.

My father was within alone, sitting by the light of one taper and the dim glow from the untended fire.

'Is that thee, Mall?' he said, looking up.

'Yes, Father,' I answered, propping my crook by the door and coming to his side. He rose up, and put his arm around me. 'Thou art well, lass? Naught amiss?'

'Why, what should be amiss, father?' I said. 'I am well. Let me put supper on the fire. Where has my mother gone?'

'She is comforting Widow Cooper, Mall. Young Edward Cooper is dead.'

'Oh, no, father, no, he cannot be!' I cried. 'He was well and laughing this very morn, and walked a way with me!'

'He is fallen sick, and was dead within the hour, Mall, believe me.'

'Oh, no! Oh, no, dear God!' I said. 'I must go down at once, I must bring some help . . . I must go!'

'No, daughter. Thy mother bade me prevent thee. There is danger enough to her in going to help the Coopers, and that peril she would not have thee share. It was the Plague, Mall. The boy died with the plague-tokens on him, and, it now seems, the tailor had them also. Now God have mercy on us all; and most solemnly I do forbid thee, Mall, to enter the Coopers' cottage, or go near any of that kin.'

'I have this day borrowed a Bible of her, father, that I must return . . .'

'Mall, thou art our only child. Do as I have asked. I will take back the Bible for thee . . . there, now, do not weep . . . I will bring supper to the table, do not mind . . .'

So I sat down at the hearth, and watched my father putting the pot to the fire, and bringing the bread, and such tasks as he never set his hand to before, as far as I could remember. I thought of the poor callow boy who had blushed, and doted, and promised me Bakewell pies, and come glowing with youth and health with me up the street in the morning . . . I could have afforded him a little kindness . . . I was shaking from head to foot, as though I had been dropped into cold water, and weeping so fast my cheeks burned, and the firelight smeared and wavered as though I had seen it through water.

In a while my father put a shawl round me, and led me to my bed.

It was not named abroad for many days. Though my father had called it Plague that struck down poor Edward Cooper, though my mother and Mistress Cooper had seen upon the tailor and upon Edward's body that which they knew it by, they said nothing of what they knew, but hoped in God's mercy it would quickly pass. So it was called 'the sickness'. And it was nothing wonderful to have a sickness in the town; there are many sicknesses, and never a year in which a sickness does not carry men, women and children to God. There is a winter sickness that makes the gaffer and the gamma cough and die, however careful of their safety their children and grandchildren are; there is a summer sickness that comes with a spotted face and burning fever, and takes off the children from one day to the next. There is a sickness from drinking foul water, and one from eating foul meats, and on, and on – only Goody Trickett could name them all over for you, and offer remedies for some, though for others help is there none to be given. There is neither an apothecary nor a surgeon in Eyam; so for what Goody Trickett and her garden of herbs cannot heal we trust to God. Except that the farrier can set a broken bone on man or horse.

The day after Edward Cooper, the sickness took Peter Halksworth, that lived next door; then three days and there died Thomas Thorpe, and his wife Mary was lying so ill she could not follow the coffin to the grave, and Sarah Sydall, Emmot's youngest sister, was lying ill also. Sydalls lived the other side the street from the cottage row where Coopers and Halksworths dwelt, but nearly facing.

The houses are set close together there, to the west of the churchyard, above the Inn. Left and right of the street they crowd up close, until you reach the river on one side and the stocks on the other, and there is some open space and room between one dwelling and the next. It was all in the middle part of the street that the sickness spread grievously. A path was newly beaten along by the back of the street and into the top of the churchyard from the open hillside, for none would so much as pass through the village street by the infected houses, being afraid of taking contagion from the air. And by the time Mistress Cooper's other son, young Jonathan, was laid beside his brother, which was the twenty-eighth day of October, there had been twenty-five of our neighbours buried, out of six families. There were some Torres lost, whom I had thought to have had as kinsfolk, they being cousins to Thomas; but poor Emmot Sydall had lost her father, her brother, and her four younger sisters, and not all that my father could say could keep my mother and me from going to Sydalls' – my mother to her mother, and I unto Emmot.

Though many of their sometime friends avoided them, hastening past them in the street and stepping never across the threshold of their house, Roland Torre had come up from Middleton bringing once his mother and father. Emmot's mother in her sorrow talked on of the hope of Roland and grandchildren to comfort her. And Emmot talked in like wise to me. We sat at her casement, closed against the autumn wind, but bringing the brightness of the sun for it looked south, and we could see from it the treetops of the woodland dell below the town.

'Come, Mall, make a charm with me,' she said on a time, brightening a little. 'I heard that to put a sixpence in the Book of Ruth, and to put the Bible beneath the pillow and to sleep, is to dream of who will be husband. And see, I have found and kept a sixpence to try it.'

'Oh, Emmot, should we?' I asked, ill at ease, looking at the black band upon her sleeve, and thinking of so many of her family so lately laid to rest.

'Oh, Mall!' she cried, 'I cannot bear it! I shall go mad with all this weeping and talk of death! Am I to have no joy ever again while I live? Thinking of Roland buoys my spirits up, and this charm will make me dream of Roland, Mall.'

'There is no truth in charms, Emmot, as I think, and this one but fond maid's foolishness.'

'It is upon the Bible, Mall.'

'And may be the worse for that. Try it if thou wilt, Emmot, when I am gone home again.'

'It will show me Roland, Mall. It *must* show me Roland. But I am afraid to try it when I am alone. Please, Mall.'

So I consented, for I saw it helped her sadness. She needed me to find the Book of Ruth, and she set a sixpence in the pages, and closed the book upon it, and set it beneath the pillow of her bed. Then we two lay down upon the bed, and leant our heads side by side upon the pillow, but we were not soon asleep. Little wonder, in broad day! We whispered together; and Emmot would have had me tell her if Thomas had kissed me yet, full upon the lips, and I would not say. But we drowsed off at last, with the warmth of ourselves fully clad, and lying close under the coverlet.

And I dreamed bright and clear. I dreamed of the day in the snows of April, when I drew forth the lamb for Thomas in the deep cavern of the drift. Each moment I dreamed very slow, so that Thomas walked forever towards us in the sun, and pulled me and Francis forever back towards his ewe. The dream had remembered how tall Thomas stood that time, over my head, when I was but a child. And all the time I dreamed I saw not Thomas's face, for it was deep shadowed under the brim of his hat; but as I woke I saw the boy's face of Francis Archdale, who had brought me home to the townhead.

I reckoned little of this charming for aught it had done for me; but I had no leisure to think of my dream, for I woke to Emmot weeping and beating the pillow with her fists, and I was hard put to it to calm her frenzy. I guessed full easily that she had not dreamed of Roland; but of what she had dreamed she could not say for tears.

'Why, Emmot, what an evil turn we have done ourselves, playing on ourselves so ill a trick!' I said. 'This was all foolishness, and well enough if it served to comfort thee, and not worth a pinch of feathers else.' I spoke many words before she ceased to weep. Poor girl, she had enough cause for weeping without any dreams. At last she grew quiet, and she told me she had dreamed her mother left her, and went away to live in a hollow cave in the dellside. She was left all alone in the dark, and could not find a taper nor a spark of light.

'Well, we have learned our lesson, Emmot,' I said. 'Let us resolve to play at charms no more.'

'Art thou certain they are folly, and bring no truths to light, Mall?'

'I am certain of it. This serves only to fright us.'

'Would it help if we put the sixpence in the poor-box, now?'

'That must needs do some good,' I said.

'Take it, and put it in,' she said, giving me the coin.

'Give it yourself, Emmot,' I said.

'I do not like to go out and into church, Mall,' she said, 'to see folk shrink from me and turn away.'

'Then I will take it for you,' I said.

My mother and I stepped across the road to the church

and I put Emmot's sixpence in the box, and then we would have gone, but the new Parson Momphesson was there putting a white cloth upon the altar, it then being Saturday, ready for the service on the morrow.

'You have been visiting Sydalls' house,' he said to us. 'You should have a care.'

'Do you tell us not to visit our neighbours in their affliction?' my mother said. Her voice was very low, but I knew her to be angry.

'There is peril in it,' he said. 'The sickness among us is the Plague. I have seen the unmistakable tokens of it upon the dying.'

'And shall folk die, and grieve without comfort, alone, here in Eyam, as in a savage land?' my mother said.

'I will go in and minister to them. It is my duty. But you, good Mistress Percival, and your daughter may have a care, and look to your own safety.'

'It is the duty of all Christian people,' she answered him, ice cold, and angry yet.

He opened the church door for her to go out. 'Could not Mistress Sydall and her daughter sit with you at the hearth in your goodly house, in the clean air of the upper town, better than you all sitting in the contagious spot?' he said to her. 'Comfort may be given as well in your house as in hers.'

And when my mother, on reaching home, told over this talk to my father word for word, and in a fine rage about it, he said it was the first morsel of sense he had yet heard of from the new parson's lips.

Now word was out it was the Plague we had; such secrets do not keep for long. Folk took fright at it. On the morrow of the day when my mother had been offended at Parson Momphesson's counsel, we were awoken from our beds by such a clattering and to-do in the street as we had seldom heard; and going to the casements and brushing off the breath-dew upon the glass, we saw three empty carts going up the town. As we took breakfast there came a neighbour to tell us that they were gone up to Sheldons' Farm; and ere we were done eating the carts came down again, laden high with chests and chairs and bundles, and the baby strapped on the top of the curtain-bale, crying loud, and manservants and maidservants carrying, or driving cows, and the little boy Sheldon leading the goat, and Mistress Sheldon bearing in her arms a loudly quacking hamper of withy-weave. Even the ducks from off the pond were going away!

As you may well suppose, this noise and spectacle brought families staring into every doorway in the road; and they had their fill of it too, for at the tail of the procession came Mistress Agnes Sheldon, Farmer Sheldon's spinster sister, a deal older than he and a thorn in his flesh daily, as all the world well knew. And as she walked she railed upon him.

'Going to Hazleford, indeed!' she cried. 'Since when was Hazleford grand enough for Sheldons, may I ask?'

'Thou hadst best hold thy tongue, and come too, sister,' said Farmer Sheldon.

'Fie upon you, brother, for a cowardly man! What will the neighbours think?' cried she. And, lest we didn't think what she supposed, she continued, 'I'll tell thee – they'll wonder what evil deed is on thy conscience, brother, that thou art afraid of the Lord's vengeance! An honest man fears not the Plague, but trusts in God! Oh, thou shameful fellow, thou . . .'

'Go to, sister, go to,' he said, hanging down his head. And by now half the town was trotting along behind the trundling carts, and the shouting woman, all ears and smiles. My mother and I went along with all the rest; my father had more dignity, but he missed the best of it.

Beside the churchyard gate she baited him at last to stand at bay. 'There is a foul contagion here,' he said. 'And we are going to a place of clean airs and safety until it has passed.

And, sister, I implore thee for thy own health to come with us . . .'

'He hath another farm at Hazleford,' she told the eager crowd, 'which ever till now my lady his wife thought not fit for her – though she hath tried very hard to make me dwell in it – and now, lo! suddenly it is good enough and more. Bad conscience, bad conscience, say I! That baggage his wife hath cause to fear the Lord's displeasure, and dare not say that the righteous shall fear no ill, not she!'

'Oh, sister, for shame!' said poor Mistress Sheldon, very red. 'Thou knowest no ill of me, that you should speak of me thus.'

'Dost thou think the Lord sees not what way you treat a poor spinster aunt?' cried she. 'Dost thou think the Lord knows not what happened to my silver thimble, or who tore my stump-work box? Did not the Lord hear thee, yesterday se'ennight, what thou saidst to me?'

We overhearers were all moved to laughter, and that intemperately, till our sides would split; but, sudden, here was the old Parson Stanley, coming down the street to us.

'Agnes Sheldon,' said he, very grave and severe, 'the Lord's displeasure is not thine to bandy with. Thou dost blaspheme. Silent, woman!'

A small gleam of triumph entered the eye of the farmer's wife, and she darted a glance at her terrible sister-in-law but said not a word.

'Parson Stanley!' cried Agnes Sheldon, not a whit discomforted. 'Tell thou my fool brother and his fool wife, that the hand of the Lord will be upon Hazleford as it is upon Eyam and elsewhere, though they flee to the utmost end of England!'

'Woman, dost thou not know what word the Bible hath for him that calls his brother a fool?' said Parson Stanley. 'Let them depart if they are set upon departing, and do thou repent those wicked words, lest the vengeance thou hast laid upon another fall on thee!' And now he had her mute at last.

And then we saw sudden that Parson Momphesson had come down to the lych-gate of the churchyard, and was looking on. Farmer Sheldon turned to him and said, 'William Momphesson, you are our parson now. Will you tell me I do wrong to leave this place?'

And at that we laughed no longer, but a swift hush fell across the throng. For it seemed in the instant that the two parsons were come face to face, and like to be in dispute.

'It is but common sense and natural wit to put yourselves out of danger if you can,' Momphesson said, in his mild southern voice.

'Come then, wife,' said Sheldon. 'And, sister, come or stay as thou wilt,' and he slapped the rump of his horse at the traces of his cart, and he and all his family trundled away, and all his livestock, the most enormous quacking coming still from the hamper of ducks.

And as they went Parson Stanley spoke again. 'The rich who have another house to go to have thy blessing, Momphesson. What wilt thou say to these many poorer folk who must needs stay here where their shelter and sustenance is?'

'I will remain among them whatever befall. I will not desert them, but will do all I can. I have already written to Cambridge and to London to have whatever physic may be got,' said Momphesson.

'You will not give them any word of God, to have help to their spirit?' said Stanley.

The Sheldons' racket was drawn a little off; but we stood all so still the little singing of the trickle of water at the river yards away could be heard by all. I stood near enough the new parson to see how he clenched his fists, whitening the knuckles of them, but he answered not soon; and when he did answer his voice had not lost its mildness.

'Thou art a most learned man, Thomas Stanley,' he said.

'I am sure thou canst point me out a text for this present trouble.'

'Psalm ninety-one, Parson,' Thomas Stanley said. And he too spoke quietly.

'Yes indeed,' said Momphesson. And raising his voice he said to we all, 'Trust God, and there shall no evil befall thee, neither shall any plague come near thy dwelling, for he shall give his angels charge over thee, to keep thee in all thy ways . . .'

It was not till the evening, by the light of a tallow candle, that opening the Holy Book at ninety-one of Psalms to read as the old parson thought fit, we saw at once that the words of preaching the new parson had spoken were those of the very psalm Stanley had named: Momphesson had it by heart, word for word.

After the Sheldons left the world grew worse for Eyam. The Bradshaws left their fine half-builded hall, standing unfinished beside its finished barns, and all their masons and carpenters departed. With them went many chances for poorer folk: sales of broth and brews and salats by cottage wives, sales of parcels of nails and iron braces from the forge, work helping and making and feeding workers and setting things to rights, which had helped put groats and shillings in many plain family purses. All this ceased and left us fallen on harder times. Poor George Vicars would have found little tailoring enough, had he been still in need of any, to pay his place by the fire.

And after the Bradshaws, the Eyres and the Wrights left, so that no gentlefolk were there remaining among us. Therewith a quietness fell upon the town, deeper for that few folk sought us out. Visitors were there scarce any to Eyam, from anywhere around. Those came with work to do, like the Barmaster, seeing over the sharing of lead from the mines, but he lingered not to drink and talk in the Talbot Inn as once he would have done. The great coming and going of cousins and kindred ceased, or all but ceased; and child was carried to the font without a crowd of family thronging the church, without need of more than a jug of ale to drink its name into its family's mind.

Poor Emmot, sitting in her empty house, desolate of the voices of her brother and sisters, with only the frequent sound of weeping from her mother's chamber, had now another pain to suffer. For although Roland and his family had come up from Middleton to offer condolences, and to play the part of kindred-to-be to the Sydalls, yet when the Plague spread all about the town and the great bell tolling in Eyam church tower could be heard at Middleton every day, then Torres in Middleton became afraid for young Roland's safety and forbade him to come to Eyam.

He came once, Emmot told me, in despite of them, but then the churchwardens of Middleton called him before them and rebuked him, showing him in terrible words what it would be if he brought the sickness upon his own family and his own town, and laying threats and oaths upon him. Worse even; Roland was Mistress Sydall's best hope for her now only child; the marriage of him to Emmot was all she had in prospect, and she too became afraid that Roland would take the illness, breathing the poisoned air of Eyam, and so she too implored him to keep away and turned him from her door, bidding him come again when all was over and the sickness marched no more.

All this had no sooner happened than I heard of it, for Emmot had not strength enough to endure this last misfortune.

'Dear friend, think of it as love for him, to do without seeing him, since it is for his sake . . .' I said to her. I knew not what to say to her weeping and railing. Though she seemed to think it was only cruelty that made her mother or churchwardens whosoever think to part them, yet the sickness had been in Sydalls' house so terrible that anyone might think it prudence for Roland to keep far off, and so thought I. And naught that I could say would comfort her.

'It is well for thee, Mall,' she cried, 'to offer bitter counsel! Thy Thomas waits still for thee, every day upon the hillside! Tending sheep, forsooth!'

I had no need of Emmot to instruct me to fear for Thomas's safety. I could not persuade him to keep away from me. He could see no danger. And in truth, upon the uplands it was hard to see. The sweet winds of autumn swept across the airy plains, and over the crest of the hills plucked and roared fierce and clean. The pure air filled my lungs and flushed my cheeks, and Thomas leapt across the rough ground, whistling up his dogs and my Ranter with them, working the sheep across the pasture to the watering places, and it was hard to think some poison might cling about me and reach to Thomas.

'All blown away, love!' he called to me, laughing – though from up there, when the wind blew not from Eyam, but near always towards it, we could not hear the bell even.

The great bell of Eyam had written upon it, SWEET JESU BE MY SPEDE. And it sped many on its way, and Thomas heard it not. Neither did he see what I saw, hear what I heard, daily. He was always light of heart, and reckless of frights and fears.

The Plague which we so well learned to know had many forms and aspects, all of them terrible. Most often the stricken persons would feel ill and fevered, and betake themselves to bed. There, in a day or two, they would be afflicted with swellings of horrible size. The swellings arose in the groin of the sufferer, or in the side of the neck, so that the head was twisted over to one side, or in the armpit or, in some few, in the elbow. The swellings were tight and red and hard, and horrible sore. Sometimes the swellings would burst open and give forth a foul and stinking effusion, and if they did so then there was hope for the poor sufferer. But if the tumours broke not the fever would become worse, and the victim would bleed easily from the nose, and at last would be covered with blotches, the ill-famed plague-tokens, which were livid red marks upon their bodies like great blood-blisters beneath the skin. If the tokens were once seen, hope was there none of recovery.

Because the breaking of the swellings gave better hope, there were some who counselled scalding a knife and cutting them open as a means of helping the sick, but there were few who had courage to suffer or to inflict such a remedy.

The Plague took not always this course I have described. There were some who fell ill without swellings, but who coughed piteously till they coughed blood, and the tokens appeared clear upon them, and they died so. And there were some who were struck dead within the hour of feeling some small unease, showing no signs of sickness at all, until the shirt was taken from the corpse, and a scatter of plague-spots was seen upon them. Poor Edward Cooper died in this sudden way; and Alice Teylor too, as she was talking with the neighbours in the street, she fell suddenly dead before them, to their very great terror and amaze.

It is the nature of the Plague, also, that it disorders the senses of those who suffer it. In the first moments of its onset, the sufferer sees strange lights, or smells what is not to be smelt by any other person in the place, or hears dogs howling, or sweet voices singing, which to others are inaudible. And then, later, when the sickness is raging, the poor sufferers fall into frenzies and know not what they are doing, and in this state they will tear off their clothes, leap from their sickbeds and run roaring in the streets, and such distempers, very horrible to those who watch.

Of those who sicken of the Plague by many the most part die; and yet do some recover, so that hope abides amidst despair at their bedsides till the last gasp of breath they draw. And so I must tell of the last form in which death comes to Plague sufferers, the cruellest way of all. It befalls sometimes that the illness goes off, the fever cools, and the frenzy ceases, so that the sick person returns unto himself again, and lies smiling at the rejoicing of his dearest ones. And then, feeling no more distress, these survivors make some movement – starting up from the pillow, or wishing to trouble no more the weary kindred who have tended them, they go to creep from bed to close a casement, or reach a sip of water . . . and as they move, they die, like a candle going out in a gust. No manner of dying gave more grief to those who lived on than this.

During the time the Plague was at Eyam we sought to see what we might do to aid the recovery of the afflicted, but the knowledge escaped us. It was like grasping at mist, to try to comprehend the working of the sickness. Margaret Blackwell, for an example, lay, as her brother Anthony thought, dying, in late October; and though none would come into his house to sit with her, yet he had business in Tideswell, buying coals, that would not wait if they were not all to freeze that winter. Anthony therefore rose at dawn, put a piece of bacon on the fire for his breakfast, and ate it in haste, and was gone, thinking the sooner to be home again. Poor Margaret became afflicted with a tormenting thirst, and the frenzy was bringing and fetching her wits to and fro that she knew not what she did for three minutes together. She rose up from her bed and came to the kitchen, and found there a wooden piggin, as she thought, of clear water standing, and gulped it all down, and returned to her bed. What she had taken was not water, but the fat from the bacon. And when her brother came home, looking to find her dead, he found her sleeping easily, the sickness having left her.

On account of Margaret Blackwell a nasty pot of melted fat was offered in vain to many sick folk in Eyam; yet others, who had drunk no such potion, recovered as well as her. Much anxious talking went on among us in our trouble, as we told over what had happened to this one and to that, seeking to know what help might be found to be given, and never found we anything with any certainty.

And if we sought eagerly to know what might aid the sick, with frenzy we sought to know what might keep the sickness from us. That it was a catching illness seemed most probable; yet there were those who came and went in every afflicted house, sat by many bedsides, lanced tumours, carried away soiled linens, cared nothing for their own safety, and took no harm at all. New parson and old breathed the foul air of every sickroom, and were untouched; and others going but once to comfort a friend or neighbour seemed in a moment to be stricken, and to carry the trouble into a whole new neighbourhood. It was readily apparent that one who had suffered and recovered was less like to be smitten a second time, and more like to recover if against likelihood they were distempered twice; but that was poor comfort indeed for those still in health!

We knew not, therefore, what to do to save ourselves, and some took no care at all, saying, 'What will befall, will befall . . .', and others were afraid even to call to a neighbour across the street or so much as look upon the kindred of the sick. And they that did much to keep from catching it, and they that did naught, fell sick alike, so that there was no discerning any cause or reason in what befell, except it was the will of God, his providence and judgement upon us. And if it was indeed God's judgement, it was a judgement upon our secret hearts, for nothing the neighbours knew for or against each other's virtue would answer with the dealings of the sickness. For all that, I think it must have been God's hand; is not everything alike his doing? We must needs remember that God may carry the good early to heaven, as soon as he may dispatch the wicked into hell; and yet I think it was poisoned air also – for the very beasts took the contagion from us, as any might see, and the rats came out of their holes, and died, as thick as we.

And here I have set down all that I know of the Plague in

one place, for I know if I were to write for all my friends and neighbours, for all the children I used to play with, for each several one of them the manner of their dying, that such a one was taken thus, and another swelled up in such a wise, while his brother and his sister, and his father and mother died in another way . . . if I should try to write thus I should have no heart and stomach for it, and could not write this spelling that I have set my hand to, to any end at all, nor ever cleanse my mind of what I have seen befall so many and so beloved souls.

I resume, then, with writing that I was afraid for Thomas, that he would take the sickness from me, and that I might carry it to him, not knowing myself afflicted, so suddenly could it strike. Winter was coming upon us, the rams were out among the ewes, and I knew not how I should keep my sheep foddered and safe if I worked not with Thomas and his dogs; and I thought if I should leave them all to him, my flock and his together would be more than he could muster and tend, and dig from drifts in winter, and then I thought how he and I would meet and labour together, and I was afraid the sickness would pass from my clothes to his, my hand to his, my very breath to his, I all unknowing what I did.

So, having taken thought, I went up on the hill a day that Thomas was to market, with Ranter at my bidding running beside, and parted my sheep from his and drove mine down to Eyam, there to keep them penned. I had thought where they might be safe kept in – and that was in the barn of Bradshaw Hall, among the stored furniture and the great boxes. Half the barn was full of good hay, handy for the taking. There I would visit them, and thence I would drive them forth to graze the slopes near by, and need go never near Thomas all the long winter through.

So thought I. And when it was done my heart was very heavy, and the thought of days without sight of Thomas or word with him was on my back like a heavy burden to heave every step I took, though I was resolute and did not change my mind.

Emmot had found some calm and cheerfulness, to my surprise I do confess, and she laid no more gloom and tears on me to worsen my own lowness. I wondered if she would chide me for making bold and putting muddy beasts in the Bradshaw barn, among their finery, and indeed, 'But if they knew!' she said. 'What if thy sheep eat up those woolly pictures, Mall!'

'I purpose not to open up the store chest for them,' said I, smiling. 'Dost think I should?'

'It would serve Bradshaws right!' she said, with sudden bitterness. 'Oh, it would serve them right, coming sporting their wealth and finery before us, and then fleeing away, leaving us to suffer, while they sleep in sweet safety! Your sheep could not trample and soil enough to please *me*.' Then she smiled an odd smile, and said, 'Mall, what if they knew? If someone told them the beasts were pastured in their keeping place, what then? How they would grind their teeth! But would they come back to keep their goods from harm? Not they, I'll wager; they would just lie awake, fretting, and afraid to come again. That would be a fine spite on them!'

'Why, Emmot,' I said, sharing her smile at this thought, 'I trust 'tis only of their hay my sheep will make some ruin; but were it otherwise, there is no way to send the news after them.'

'They are not gone so far . . .' she said; and then, 'No, of course not.'

'But if you had, Emmot,' I said, a little troubled at her, 'I pray you tell not my name as the owner of the trampling flock.'

She smiled at me slyly, and said, 'Would I breed trouble for you, Mall? But gladly would I spite them!'

While we were talking thus we heard laughter in the street outside. Laughter that had been as common in Eyam as wind-sighs in the leaves, or the trickle of streams, had faded so away that autumn that hearing it was a singular thing, and brought us at once to the threshold to look out and see.

There coming up the street in a line were a dozen or so ducks, the most miserable, sodden, dejected fowl that ever I saw, and scarce able to waddle another step, so it seemed. Behind them came children, pointing and laughing. And young women though we were, Emmot and I, we fell in line behind the children, and followed up the street, arm in arm, under a bruised grey sky and in a cold wind. The ducks at last reached Sheldons' pond, and with feeble quacks and splashes launched onto it; whereupon out of her door came Mistress Agnes, calling down blessings and scattering grain, declaring that any one of the wanderers returned was worth two and three of her brother and sister-in-law for grace and sense, and knowledge of the ways of the Lord. Most providential and pious ducks, to walk home from Hazleford! Eggs and feathers, eggs and feathers for Agnes, who trusted God and God had given the ducks back to her, praise him in all his ways!

And when she had thrown half a bushel of grain at the ducks she handed out lardy-cake to every one of us who stood laughing at her, with a good deal of talk about the Lord's providence for us, too.

The day after Sheldons' ducks came home their pond was frozen iron-hard, and none but Marshall Howe was hefty enough to break it for them. And at nightfall the snow came on. It was early for heavy snow – the second day of December only, but it fell and fell, and laid down near three foot thick on everything. My father was glad of it, he supposing from what he had been told the pestilence would abate in cold weather, and perhaps leave us. Yet there died nine in that snow-girt December, there having been seven in November which was wet and mild. And for everyone buried there was another fell sick. It was but a sad Christmas we had. And at the turn of the year there had been forty-five dead, out of the small number in this our little town. And the newest into the ground was Anthony Blackwell, he of the bacon breakfast, Margaret's brother, who died on Christmas Eve.

Yet it was cold enough for anything. The springs were frozen; Tricketts' cow died against a hedge in a field. Fiddler's Brook froze to the mud, and the boys took fish up out of it in blocks of ice. I had needs make free with Squire's hay to feed my flock, there being no grass for them to graze upon, and ever in my mind was the thought of Thomas, striving with his much greater flock, alone on the waste of snow on the icy windswept hill.

In time of trouble the people turn for comfort and for counsel to the clergy; and we had not one but two parsons to whom to turn, but they spoke not with one voice.

Thomas Stanley our old parson was forbidden by law to preach to us now, and he stood not in pulpit nor in the street to speak, but people sought him out, asking him for his words. In the garden of that house whereto he had removed, all those of the old way of thinking, we Puritans, would forgather on Sunday at dusk. We would hear the Bible, and Thomas Stanley would teach us and speak to us. Anyone might have denounced him for doing this, and had him hailed forth by force away from us to terrible punishment, but none had yet done so at the time of which I now write.

And there was comfort in what Parson Stanley said. 'No sparrow falls,' he taught us, 'except by the will of God. And we stand all every hour in the immediate providence of God, and draw not one breath save by his will. Those wicked men whom he hath chosen to punish, and those good men whom he hath chosen to try by suffering, as he tried Job of old, will find death and sickness. But the disease

61

cannot of itself spread among us, for not a hair of our heads can be touched except by God's will. Refrain not therefore from visiting the sick; draw not back your hand from their very sores, there will no harm befall those who have faith. Put no trust in sweeping the house clean, or in burning herbs, or suchlike idleness, but repent your sins, and have faith in the Lord. Listen, and I will read to you what hath been promised to us by our God.'

So stood we under the snow-laden boughs, under a cruelly frosty sky, our shawls clutched close about us and our breath in drifts of mist by moonlight and torchlight, and heard him read to us, in his strong, faithful voice:

'Because Thou hast made the Lord, even the most High thy habitation,

'There shall no evil befall thee, neither shall any Plague come nigh thy dwelling,

'For He shall give his angels charge over Thee, to keep thee in all thy ways.

'Thou shalt not be afraid of the terror by night, nor for the arrow that flieth by day, nor for the pestilence that walketh in darkness, nor for the destruction that wasteth at noonday.

'A thousand shall fall at thy side, and ten thousand at thy right hand, but it shall not come nigh thee ...'

We were comforted hearing this. And with a right strong believing, I believed it, until ... I run forward, setting things down out of good order...

I resume. When someone asked Parson Stanley why God's displeasure and his justice were heavy upon us, so many of us, he answered very sorrowfully that he feared that the Plague of God was in the land for the new mixture of religion that was commanded in the church. And still all who heard him were comforted; for those of us who stood in the bitter cold to hear him were those who much misliked the changes, and would fain have kept the old ways of worship still, and so we surely stood in less danger than those folk of Eyam whose hearts went with the changes!

In altogether a different sense did our new parson speak. True, Parson Momphesson also bade us repent our sins and throw ourselves upon God's mercy. He reminded us, but in a gentle tone, that some had made a mockery of God's holy service, bringing a poor dumb beast within the sanctuary – and how had he learned of that? we wondered – there were hard hearts among us, that would not give credence to God's sacraments. All this we should repent, and our kindly Father in heaven would turn aside his wrath.

But he told us also we must not tempt God; we must not ask his help while neglecting what we could do to help ourselves. He told us therefore that we must not enter the houses of the sick, unless it were having some most pressing need – to give physic, perhaps. We who had, he said, no duty to risk ourselves should keep away and leave it to him, upon whom the duty fell, to go in and minister comfort to the sick. He had got physics up from London, he told us, which he would bring to any who had need; he had heard that burning bunches of herbs would cleanse the air of contagion, and urged us to purify our houses with this remedy; he told us to bury our excrement in a deep pit some distance from the house, and likewise any other foulness from kitchen or sickroom, and for the time being to cast no such matter forth into the street. Moreover we should be sure to drink clean water. Eyam being blessed with its several clear running streams, all that was needful was for us to draw it, and carry it in clean vessels. And we should find courage to bear our tribulations with patience.

There were very few of us who liked his words. Burning of herbs and suchlike seemed but a poor help against so great a peril. And though it was in great fear that we crept in to visit friends lying sick, yet still we thought it was our duty to do so. And should most Eyam folk heed Parson Momphesson, then it should be our turn to lie tossing and burning on a pallet all alone, and none would come nigh to aid us, in our turn; a prayer from the new parson might not console us for the lack of water, or a clean bedcover, or a draught of Goody Trickett's herb tea!

And it was apparent, moreover, to us all that what he would not have us do, his Catherine did daily; for she went up and down the town, into any house where someone was lying stricken, bringing little messes of good food and dabs of Parson Momphesson's London liniments, and any such help she could. So that in the end Parson Momphesson accused her of being of Parson Stanley's mind.

This next I had from Mary Gregory, who was of an age with me, and played with me of old, and who came and went to our house often as a trusted friend, and who was the Momphessons' maidservant since their coming into Eyam. Their manservant they had brought with them, and he kept his own counsel so that naught could be learned from him. But Mary told us that the parsonage was a most quiet place, with never a word raised in anger or reproach, and that she had to knock at any door before entering, even the withdrawing-room, where the parson kept his books and papers, lest she come upon the parson and his wife with their arms round one another.

So, Mary said, when she heard them quarrelling she was quite set back by it. Their voices were so loud, she said, she could not help but hear, but she blushed a little saying this so that I guessed that she had had her ear next the keyhole when she overheard so much.

The parson was saying, Mary told us, 'My dove, thou shalt go no more into the people's houses.'

'I must in all things obey you, William,' she said. 'But I should be sorry to be commanded thus.'

'But so I do command thee,' he said.

'Do not so,' said she. 'In pure Christian charity should I not bring what help I can to so great afflictions?'

'Thou dost venture every time what is more dear to me than life,' said he. 'Catherine, if thou comest to any harm . . .'

'God will keep me,' she said.

'Why, Catherine,' he said, 'art thou of one mind with that wicked Puritan, who persuades the people to be so reckless of their safety and upon whose words will lie the blame for many deaths? Wouldst thou step off a tall cliff, crying that God will keep thee? Or hold thy hand in the fire, saying that the righteous need fear no evil? How then wilt thou go into the pestilential air of these narrow houses, saying "God will keep me!" like a prating Puritan?'

'Then,' said Mary, 'she answered very low – but it happened I could hear her in despite of that, "Alas, William, what terror is in thy words! What terrors do surround us! Let us go hence together, William, on the instant! See, on my knees I do implore thee, remove thyself and us while there is yet time to flee away unscathed!"

'"My dear, I cannot go," he said, in a most troubled and afflicted voice. "My duty is here, with these people. God knows, and you know, I did not wish to come here; God knows and you know what a divided and uncertain welcome I have found. But I am their pastor, and I will be pastor to them to the limit of my powers. But thou art not likewise placed, Catherine. It would be good wisdom if thou didst take up the children and remove to a safer place..."

'"No, William," she answered. "If thou stay, I stay. For my life, I would not leave thee."'

There was a silence then, and Mary heard nothing, and could not see through the door. She supposed they were embracing. Then Catherine said, 'I shall remain here while you remain, William. But our sweet babes – could we not send them hence a while?'

'They would be safe in Yorkshire,' he replied. 'If thou canst bear to part with them, Catherine, we will send them out of danger on the first possible occasion.'

'Thou wilt forgive me if I weep to see them go,' she said.

'But I would not keep them at my side to give me joy at hazard of their lives!'

'So say I of thee, Catherine.'

'But I will not go.'

'Well then, if thou remain, go thou no more into the houses of the sick; keep thyself out of harm's way, for my sake.'

'I am loth to obey thee in this,' she said. 'Abiding here, and hearing tell of all this dolefulness, and doing nothing of kindness, is a hard conduct. But as you are my husband, I will obey.'

'And the poor duck,' said Mary, telling me and many more all about it, 'lay weeping in her chamber a full hour after this. And when she called me to bring her a sip of milk and set the children's supper upon the table, her eyes were red and swollen that badly!'

'Truly, she is a merciful and kind lady,' my mother said. 'But she had best heed her husband. She is not of a strong constitution, and think you not, she might take sick easily.'

'Thou hast the right of it, neighbour,' said Mary. 'She has often a dry cough, which never seems quite to go, and she is thin – a deal too thin.'

Again my story runneth all awry. I resume: we had two parsons, and they taught us differently. Some inclined to one and some to the other. Only my father railed on both holy men. 'Is it the cow in church hath brought us low?' he asked. 'But Marshall Howe's rascally son was the ringleader in that, and he walks hale and hearty, while others who had no part in it lie dead. Is it the changes in the service book? And has Eyam alone, then, in all this part of England, changed its ways? Why die they not in every place in Derbyshire, but only here?'

'But, father, then, what do you think the cause?' I asked him. I was loth to leave off believing Parson Stanley, for repentance was a thing possible to me, and I clung to the hope of safety promised upon it.

'Child,' he said to me, 'if none know a thing, and none can know it, it were best none claimed to know it. I will tell you this, child, I would not soon trust my safety in a lead mine to the providence of God; I would sooner trust my own contriving, my own care to study cracks, and put props to the roof.'

My mother rebuked him then. 'Dost thou think God's might goeth not underground?'

'It may be that God's providence runs everywhere,' he said. 'But there is no understanding it.'

It was a hard winter. I was thankful full often that my ewes were near by, penned in. I went up the snow-filled street to them at dawn and at nightfall every day, to bring them water and fresh hay. My father grumbled at my going on thus; he said often that I had no need, that I should keep my hands clean, and my mind on learning reckoning. Yet when last year I sold my clip at Tideswell Fair and brought home a purse of silver for my good wool, he said that not a man in Eyam had a son the worth of his daughter, and not a man in Derbyshire would be worthy of her to wife. And he was glad enough of the good cloak I made him from my own wool, and my own spinning, and poor George Vicars' making up. 'Neither wool nor mutton are got without labour in winter weather, father,' I told him, and I still set forth.

I came once at dusk, and saw a light already shining in the barn. I wondered at it, and went hastily in. There was Thomas, on his knees, at work with the oldest ewe; the poor beast miscarrying her lamb.

'Go home, Thomas!' I said. 'You are in peril here. And flocks of your own you have in plenty, that need your aid.' But my voice took the colour not of my meaning, but of my poor heart, overjoyed to see him.

'This will take both of us, Mouse,' he said. 'Hold her head. Be quick – no disputation!'

For all that we could, we lost the ewe that night. When she was dead Thomas clipped her coat, and rolled it up for me, and asked me did I want also the skin, but I could not bear to see it taken, in my distress for the loss of the beast.

'This loss you can well sustain, Mall,' Thomas said, as we sat wearily on the straw. 'You have been doing well enough. Wilt have a bite of my pasty for sustenance?'

'How do you know how well I have been doing, Thomas?' I asked.

'I have been by some few times,' he said, 'and looked how things were with your sheep. Tonight when I found something amiss I waited for thee.'

'Thomas, you must not come.'

'Sayst thou so, Mouse? Dost not love me, then?'

'Is it not love that makes me fear for thy safety, coming so near?'

'I cannot endure being parted from thee,' he said. 'Let me come. Or come thou away with me.'

'And if I come with thee, and coming bring the sickness into Wardlow, and suffering such as we have seen in Eyam comes into your parish also – what then?'

'Thou dost not look sick to me, Mall, thou of the light tread, and the rosy cheek, and shining eyes. Kiss me, Mouse.'

'Thomas, I have seen a boy well one moment, and dead the next. I could be in full vigour while we talk, and fall dying at the roadside in the short walk home. It is not a thing to take lightly, Thomas . . .' I shivered a little, for the truth was I was afraid. I was afraid for myself, as well as for him.

'It is hard,' he said.

'Why, if even that scatterbrain Emmot Sydall can possess herself in patience, parted from Roland, surely we can endure it!' I said.

'Ah, but she sees him every day,' Thomas said. 'Knew

you not? She slips through the woods from the bottom of her garden into the slopes of the Cucklett Dell, and he waits for her there. His family know not of it, and hers neither, I do believe. And, Mall, this is a secret – thou shalt not tell.'

'But I will try what I can to stop her, lest she brings ruin to Middleton as you would do to Wardlow. Oh, how can she? And the Plague has been in her house, and she hath seen it!'

'Perhaps she loves Roland too well to drive him off,' said Thomas. 'Perhaps she loves Roland more than thou lovest me.'

Then I said, 'Thomas, if I must choose between losing all my joy in thee, and thy safety, it is thy safety I will choose. Far would I rather thou wast living in another girl's arms than dying in mine!' The tears ran down my cheeks as I spoke to him.

He was silent a long moment. Then he said, 'There will be no other girl, Mall. Though the Plague last a hundred years, yet thou wilt find me, the day it is over, an old man still unmarried, waiting for thee on the Wardlow road!'

'Pray it be not so long!' said I. 'Begone now, love, and farewell, come no more!'

I went the next day to visit Emmot. And to her I said that it was no love she showed unto Roland, if she risked taking the Plague to him. Then Emmot wept. 'Mall, I cannot do without I see him,' she said. 'And all that we contrive is, he stands upon one rock, and I upon another, and so we talk.'

'And never tempted to lay hands or cheeks together?' I doubted.

'Why, Mall, the Plague has no power to spread all by itself,' she said. 'Only if God will it can it touch anyone; and if God wills it, what will it help not to kiss sweethearts on parting?'

'Art thou not afraid, Emmot?' I asked.

'Mortally!' she said. 'But you cannot gainsay what I have said, Mall Percival, for it is what Parson Stanley teaches. Therefore I see Roland, and I keep a careful watch upon my deeds and thoughts, and I trust God.'

'What harms will flow from it, if Parson Stanley in this be wrong!' I said, thinking aloud.

'Why should he be?' Emmot asked.

'Well, Emmot, you were little disposed to think him right when he spoke against ribbons on dresses and girls dancing with boys at the Wakes,' I said, trying to make her smile.

'But he is a virtuous and learned man, Mall,' she said, her speech eager and her face grave, 'who has spent a whole life reading and thinking on such things. And should he not be right sooner than a young man with rich friends, who dresses his child like a lady's maid, and his wife like a light-of-love, and himself wears lace to his cuffs, and drinks wine at his table; and with but a few summers' advantage over you and me, Mall, sets out to teach us what we must or must not do?'

'I think we must try to think well of both parsons, as far as we may,' I said.

'Do thou so, goody Mall,' she said. 'But I will hearken unto the old parson, for myself.'

So I saw I could not keep her from her ways, and I took my leave of her with a heavy heart.

I was used to think of myself as very well able to decide a matter better than Emmot Sydall, and yet she left me troubled. For that pain I laid upon Thomas, and that I suffered myself seeing him not, until the Plague was gone, could it be all in vain? And yet from many instances it would seem that going near one with the sickness on them, one was like to take sick oneself.

It was in the miserable wet and cold of February that something happened which set us talking for a day or two. It seemed that a carter living in Bubnell was given an order

70

for a load of logs to be delivered to Eyam. The logs were for Momphessons' fires, so it was said. So this man's neighbours, hearing that he was to go to Eyam, most heartily implored him not to, and he would not heed them at all, but for the sake of the fourpence he would earn he set out for Eyam with his cart loaded, in foul weather.

It rained on the carter all the miles to Eyam, and he was wet enough before he trundled up the deserted street. Bridget Teylor and others heard the cart wheels, and came to their windows, looking out. The carter stopped and called, and none answered him – a boy who was abroad ran, instead, full tilt away. He could find none to tell him where the parson's house might be, and none to set hand to his load to help him, but seeing him a stranger, putting himself in peril, all Eyam folk kept behind closed doors. The carter cursed most horribly, Bridget said, and drawing his cart up near the churchyard wall, set to unload the logs himself, during which hour, for so much it took him, the rain came still pelting down upon him, and the wind blew hard off Eyam Edge. At last he had shed the last log into the street, and he walked his horse up to the stocks to have room to turn the cart around, and took himself home.

When he had gone, the neighbours in that part came forth exclaiming, and Marshall Howe, coming upon a cluster of neighbours chatting by the log pile, said in a swaggering tone that had *he* but known it, he would have helped unload; whereupon everyone else berated him for his folly.

And in the midst of this, Parson Momphesson came forth and said, his logs now being piled into the road, let anyone take of them who had need, so long as they lasted, for it could not be easy to get loads delivered to us now. And hearing Marshall Howe bullying away, with his loudness, and his run-a-gate dauntless talk, he said unto him, very quiet, 'If indeed thou art without fear, Marshall, wilt thou then dig a grave for Thomas Wilson, and bring him forth from his cottage, and lay him therein? He is the last of his family.'

'Why, then,' said Marshall, 'what of Adam Halksworth?' For Adam was the gravedigger of Eyam.

'He is dead, and buried this past hour,' said Parson Momphesson. 'I ask thee to fill his office, since hearing you declare you have no fear.'

'Trust me for it!' said Marshall brazenly, 'I'll make a hole and tip 'un in for you to pray over by evening, Parson!'

And this I had from Goody Trickett, who saw it all, having run out into the street to gossip over the load of logs with her neighbours.

Meanwhile the carter went home to Bubnell, and being there fell to shivering and sneezing, and having the sweats, and a burning forehead, and his neighbours all taking fright, and fearing he had brought the Plague, nailed up his door with baulks of wood and set a watchman with a blunderbuss ready to shoot him if he came forth. His wife and child were within, locked up also, and no food was in the house so that he was driven to plead for mercy from an upstairs casement.

And it seemed this caused such a to-do in Bubnell that the great Duke himself, the Duke of Devonshire, who dwells in the palace at Chatsworth, got to hear of it, and sent forth his own doctor to look to the carter and see if it was indeed the Plague that he had. Yet the doctor had no wish to go near the patient, by any wise, and so went down to the east bank of the river Derwent, and summoned the carter to come and stand upon the west bank, and so calling across the water questioned him about his disease. Very soon the doctor knew that nothing worse than a chill was amiss, most like from taking such a soaking in the rain, and so he set the carter free from confinement.

And all this story I learned from Parson Momphesson, later in our tribulation, when he told it to us from letters he had had, to prove that other men than he might look to

72

precautions for safety, and that the Duke might concern himself with us, though it were for the first time.

The cold lay long upon the land, that we would have welcomed it only if it stemmed the Plague, and still it lingered, and still people died. The seventh day of April was the first day that the air softened, and the warmth drew people out of their houses and set them opening casements and propping doors ajar. The leaves and flowers which had been late came on suddenly apace, and the gardens and woodland floors broke into aconite, and Lent lily, and dog violet and primrose, all at once. My sheep were set free, and driven up onto the upland. I knew well they would mix with Thomas's, all bred together as they were, but I hoped I might keep from coming near him, with good care, and the ewes needed fresh grass to make milk for their lambs, of which two were come already and more expected in short time.

The softer weather now upon us, Parson Momphesson began to strive and busy himself, and ask for labour from his parishioners. He brought about the building of pest-houses on the common, well away from the traffic of the town. Not one large hospice, wherein one might take fright at the sufferings of another, but little booths, of good timber, thatched thick and flag-floored, and lime-washed within, to which the sick might be carried to lie till they recovered or died, out of the way of others of their kin. Six of these little booths were built, spaced out along the commonside. The carpenter made pallets for them out of wood and rope cording; and the parson taught that no bedding should be carried back into the houses that had been used in the plague-huts, but it should all be burnt. But the sick shivered piteously in their seizures, and whatever friend was sent to watch over them brought covers to keep them warm. And then the burning of good woollen blankets was little to the liking of the wives of Eyam.

The parson had intended that the sick only should be removed some way, but many folk in good health took occasion to remove themselves. A good number of families built themselves summer-houses on the Edge, or carried their beds and cooking pots to the caverns which pierce the cliff on either side the Delph, the Delph being a wooded deep ravine which runs down from the brink of the town street to the Dale brook, and the road to Middleton. John Merril took his cock and hens and went right up upon the crest almost of Sir William Hill, and camped there all alone. While all this cutting timber and building and carrying chattels was afoot, my father would have taken us also a small remove to a summer-house, but my mother would have none of it. Like Agnes Sheldon, she thought it showed bad conscience to flee away; she trusted God and her clear conscience for her life. And I think my father did not know what hurt to my mother's pride it would have been to leave her scrubbed kitchen, and her scoured pans and bowls, and her slate floor washed with skimmed milk once a week, and betake herself to a cave or hut like a vagabond wife!

Meanwhile the parson's huts were soon in use. In April Mary Heald, who had fallen ill soon after nursing her brother, was carried into one of them, and died there; but none other of her family died, from the large house in the Lydgate, though she had a husband and five children who might have caught it from her. And Marshall Howe fell ill. His face and armpits swelled, but none carried him any-where – he walked to the common himself, roaring and cursing horribly all the way, and lay down in one of the huts, while Joan his wife tried to bring help to him but was driven off by threats and curses. It was from heaving and burying the dead that Marshall Howe had caught it, we all supposed. But after five days he recovered, and walked back into town, with his flesh and clothes hanging loose upon him, shouting for meat and drink, and amazing all the town.

So this is how things stood with us when Saint Mark's Eve drew near.

It seems to me, looking back, that all the time Thomas Stanley was our parson he laboured like a gardener to weed out idle folly and superstition from our minds. He plucked the laces and ribbands from our dresses, and the faith in charms, and the help of saints, and mumble-jumble recitations and suchlike from our hearts. And now his hand was stayed these rank weeds started up again, and flourished. It should have been the new parson's business to root them out again, but the new parson, with his white cloth upon the altar, and bowing the head at the name of Jesus, and blessing the bread and wine, and such things, seemed to many of us not the enemy of superstition but rather a fair wind to its spreading and seeding among us. This I do know, that we began to hear tell of many superstitions, which I, being young, could never remember before having been talked of in my life, for Parson Stanley had driven them underground. As, for example, that the Plague, devilish though it was, yet had a saint all its own, one Saint Roche, whose name but written on a piece of paper and eaten – yes *eaten* – would keep a body from harm. Saint Roche, it seemed, back in King Henry's time had had a shrine on the wayside, on the road to Hazleford – I cannot for my life think who could have remembered that! So a bare spot on the parish boundary, beside a spring, blossomed suddenly with flowers laid there as offerings. Had this been but girls' foolishness it had not been so strange. Girls I think always toy with such matters, more than half in jest, dreaming of husbands and fortune. As I have written, the use of a sixpence in the Bible, or a script as a ridding charm, was well enough known to me. But when our elders and betters, sober men old enough to be grandfathers, began to talk of such things, that seemed strange indeed. The world was full of prodigies!

And it seemed that once, way back, it had been thought that anyone who kept watch by the church door all night, and until dawn on Saint Mark's Eve, would see pass through the apparitions and semblances of all who would die in the parish in the year following, until the next Saint Mark's Eve. Then some of the miners were drinking in the Talbot Inn a day or two before Saint Mark's, and they set each other on with pledges and boasts, as to who would dare sit within the porch and watch. When it came to the sticking point, as I heard – and this I had from poor Joaney Hodge who feeds her children by washing jugs and mugs in the Talbot, and fetching and carrying there – there were none of these tipsy miners ready to undertake the business, till they took a clutch of straws round and Peter Ashe drew the cut one. Peter Ashe was of about fifty summers, a strong and diligent miner, with two sons and a daughter grown up, and one with whom my father made bargains, and for whom he would advance money.

That he was about to keep watch for ghosts was soon known up and down the town. My father was sorely troubled by it, and I baffled that he should be so.

'Father, you cannot give credit to such a story,' I said.

'I would indeed have thought my neighbour Ashe would have more sense by far,' he said.

'No, I do not mean, you do not credit that Master Ashe will sit down and watch all night; I mean, you do not surely credit that if he doth, he will see ghosts afoot?'

'Twittle-twattle!' said my mother stoutly. 'That he will not!'

'And if he see no ghosts, he can come to no harm worse than to take a chill,' said I.

'I mislike it much,' my father said. 'It does not do to meddle with suchlike things. Not only because they were false were these old fancies driven out among us, but because they were perilous. I have tried to talk Peter out of

76

it, but he would sooner put his soul at risk than back down and be called a cowherd by his drinking-cronies.'

I wondered much that my father should have put himself to the trouble of talking to Peter Ashe on such a matter, and all in vain!

However, Saint Mark's Eve came, and drew towards dusk. Peter Ashe drank very deep in the Talbot until the innkeeper put up his shutters for the night, and then went across the road, his friends going with him through the lych-gate and into the porch. And there they left him, jesting as they went off. All honest folk were abed and sound asleep, and no light showed anywhere at such a time below the stars, but for the dim lantern light in an upper casement of the little house where Parson Stanley read and prayed. Although a half of Eyam at least knew what was afoot, it seemed that no one had told either parson, parson old or parson new, what Peter Ashe would do; and Peter himself in his cups had declared that he feared Parson Stanley coming with ferocious sermon to chase him forth, more than he feared whatever else might come.

At four of the clock Peter's daughter came to him, walking alone down the dark street, and trembling across the moonlit churchyard, bringing him a hot broth, and praying him to come home, and at that hour, as she later told all and sundry, he was full of cheer and courage, and laughed at her, saying he would sit it out till dawn, and make up a lying tale or two to fright the others with next day.

Thus all the hours of darkness were spun away. But when Parson Momphesson in the first beams of sunrise came through the gate from the Rectory, and through the dewy grass to the church, to his morning prayers, he found his parishioner Peter Ashe, seemingly struck stark mad, crouching in the corner of the porch, staring and shaking, and able to say one word only – 'Hundreds!'

What a to-do there was! Parson Momphesson could not prevail upon Peter to move, and at the suggestion that he should come within the church and pray with the parson, the poor man let out a wail and covered his face. Not till his daughter had been sent for, and half the townsfolk had arrived, could Parson Momphesson so much as understand what had happened; and by the time he had understood, a great press of frightened people were thronging the churchyard and pressing forward to the porch, crying out, 'Did you see me, Peter?' or, 'Did you not see . . .?' and naming all their kindred to him, while he looked so wildly, casting frantic eyes around, that everyone thought he had surely seen *them*, and still he said nothing but '*Hundreds!*'

Momphesson stood before Peter in the doorway and tried to calm the mob. 'Neighbours, this is most like what has happened. Peter here has overwatched, and at last in the dawn has fallen asleep, and since he looked to see ghosts, he has dreamed of ghosts, as any might who fell asleep thinking of them. He has frighted himself with his own folly, but there is no cause to fright you. Take yourselves off to your day's work, and pray for your foolish neighbour, rather than fear for yourselves, and make uproar!'

I am ashamed to write that none heeded his words but all called out still to Peter, and some few threatened the parson if he would not stand out of the way, and let them come to Peter, for they *would know* whom he had seen. So then some in the crowd went running to fetch the old parson and some sober men, like my father and Robert Wood, for fear folk would lay hands on the new parson, in their frenzy.

My mother and I went along with my father in haste, and when we got there I saw myself how Catherine Momphesson stood by, standing upon the stile into the churchyard, white-faced, and watching how the Eyam folk treated her husband, while Mary Gregory stood beside her on the ground, holding her fast by the hand. And as we came to the churchyard, there came old parson, Thomas Stanley also, with his son John at his side. Thomas Stanley thrust through the crowd, pushing folk out of his way, and in a great voice called, 'Peter Ashe! Thou hast done the devil's work this night, and the devil hath repaid you for it!'

'He will not go in with me and pray,' said Parson Momphesson to Parson Stanley.

'Then he shall come forth and pray with me,' Stanley replied.

'Into this furious throng?' asked Momphesson.

Whereupon Stanley turned and cried out to the people, 'Neighbours, for shame! It is the devil hath given visions here. Is the truth of any man's fate to be learned from the devil? It is all falsehood. It is not your deaths that you can discover, but your damnation you can devise by asking. Be off; be gone all!'

Even for Parson Stanley they were slow in going, and grudging, and though they moved off from the churchyard they lingered in the street.

But seeing them a little withdrawn away, Peter got up, and with one hand covering his face, and the other held out before him to grope his way, like a man blind he went towards Parson Stanley. Stanley turned and walked away, Peter following after, into the street and towards his own house. Parson Momphesson stood looking at them go. I wondered at him, seeming to bear it so calmly, being slighted once again. But Catherine jumped down from her perch, and went swiftly to his side.

At that I turned away, and followed my father and mother up the street, going home, a step behind Stanley and Peter. And as we all came up to Sydalls' house, Mistress Sydall came running forth, and seized Peter Ashe by the hand, and said to him in a shaking voice, 'Good friend, as you hope for mercy on Judgement Day, tell, tell me, did you see my Emmot's spirit, going into the church?' So swiftly did she come that Parson Stanley, turning round, was too late to stay her, as was my mother, running forward.

Peter gave no answer but a crazed stare, and a mumble without meaning, full of distress.

'Emmot?' said my father, to Mistress Sydall. 'Why should he have seen Emmot rather than any other one?'

'She is lying sick,' said Mistress Sydall, in a bare faint whisper, 'and I am afraid . . .'

'Go home, Mall, and I will help here,' my mother said.

But I was running before she had the words out, and was within the door before her sentence was finished. Up to Emmot's chamber I, and there found her flushed and burning, and a great swelling on the side of her face. I thought she could not see me, as I busied myself, though I trembled as I stepped, with bringing cool water, and making a herb broth, for her eyes were dimmed over, and cloudy. But later she said, 'Is it Mall?'

'Yes, Emmot. I am come, and thy mother is resting.'

'Be not angry with me, Mall,' she said. 'I go not to meet Roland today . . .' I thought she said, 'Or ever . . .', but her voice was dying, and perhaps she only ended with a sigh.

The days of Emmot's sickness were sore and hard for me. The lambing was upon me. Each evening I had to walk up to my flock, and drive down to the Bradshaws' barn those that looked like to lamb before morning, and rise in the night and see that they fared well. Then in the dawn I would return them to the hillside, and all this time I had to keep far from Thomas. I saw him, at work as I was at work, but I fled away if he came towards me. As soon as I could see the ewes grazing and the lambs taking suck, I would hie home again, and breaking my fast with a snatched chunk of bread and a morsel of cheese, would go out to the plague-hut where Emmot had been taken. Sending home her mother again for a rest, and more than half asleep myself, I would nod at my duty until my mother came up to take her turn and send me home again.

We both forbore to go near my father this time; he sat at

the far end of the table to his meals, and slept alone in the upstairs chamber, my mother sharing my pallet by the fire. We drank not from his cup, nor washed his platter for him, and his linen was washed by our neighbour.

I talked a little to Emmot, and read a psalm to her, when she woke, which was but seldom. The poor girl slept through her sickness like one who tosses in a bad dream; I heard her speak Roland's name, and call for her father once. She died in the night of the twenty-eighth of April, and was buried in the late afternoon the next day. Marshall Howe dug her grave, and dragged her to it on a hurdle, wrapped up in a sheet. I was dry-eyed at her graveside, because I could not weep for trembling, and in my mind I kept thinking to tell Emmot all about it, as though I could turn round and see her living, skipping along beside me, and as though she might not have heard that she was dead!

Parson Momphesson read the burial service; Parson Stanley stood at Mistress Sydall's side, and held her up while it was read, and after led her away with him to console her as best he could. And I found Bridget Teylor and Eliza Abel waiting for me at the churchyard gate as I came from thence, saying they would go with me to my sheep and keep me company if it might cheer me. They took each an arm of mine, and then I wept freely, thinking how they might have looked askance at my newer love for Emmot, when so long before I had no better friends than they, and how they might have been afraid to come nigh me, when I had been closeted with Emmot in her dying. All the way up the hill I wept, and then I found the last of my ewes to lamb already in labour, and the lamb's right hoof not showing, and that brought me quickly back to my senses, and had me hastening to work, and to telling the other two how to help me.

Thomas was nowhere to be seen that eve, and I was glad of that. I supposed he was with tending one of his own flock. It was a balmy evening, with a sweetness and a touch

81

of warmth in the air, and cooling fast under a rosy sunset. All the trees were fresh green, with tiny leaves, bright and not yet unfurled, and the yellow celandine glistened widespread in the grasses. It was not a time to die.

It was no time to die, and indeed few followed Emmot to the grave. It was a sweet fair May, full of the wild blossom and the fresh grass, and the bluebells like sky fallen in swathes across the woodland floors, and either our deep repentance or the new parson's plague-huts, or some other thing, seemed to be working, and to promise relief. For the whole month of May only four people died of Plague – two Thorpes, early in the month, James Teylor on the eleventh, and Ellen Charlsworth on the twenty-fourth. We thought the trouble was passing from us, and the disease had spent its fury, burnt itself out, like a fast fire in a small wood.

Still I kept far from Thomas, circling round him on the high hills, whistling Ranter to part my sheep from his. Thomas played games with me, shadowing me as I went upon the hillside, or bringing his flock across my homeward path, and sitting in wait for me on some knob of rock. But my eyes are as sharp as my wits, and I kept clear. He made me laugh with his tricks and stratagems to entrap me near to him, and as long as it was always I who had the best of it, and I evaded him, I was not afraid. Had he been able to come near me it would have torn my heart between longing and fear.

As May wore on I idled one afternoon, lying upon a rock in the warm sunshine, and smiling to see the lambs kick up their back legs, and jump and play. Suddenly I heard Thomas's voice, very low, and very near me! I jumped up and looked around for which way to run off; I could not see him. But he said, from behind the rock, the very rock I had just been leaning upon, 'Nay, Mouse, be still, and hold your ground. Surely the sickness strikes not through the heart of rock, and I swear I will not move from this side of it, but I *must* have words with you.'

I stood still.

'If you could see my cousin Roland, what he has become, you would have pity on him, Mall,' said Thomas, and now my heart sank like a stone in a pool.

'Word is around that only very few are dead in Eyam this month, and none this se'ennight,' said Thomas.

'That's true, Thomas,' I said. 'But the parson says it must be full three weeks, with none dead and none taking sick, before we can count ourselves clear.'

'Roland goes every day into the Dell, and Emmot comes no more to meet him there.'

That I answered not, but the tears welled up in my eyes, and ran free down my cheeks.

'He is in a frenzy of fear for her, Mall, and saying what if she be dead? But I have told him that you said you would put a stop to her coming if you could, and that perhaps if it were discovered that she came, the whole town would arise to prevent her. This I say to comfort him, Mouse, but I would fain know that this is thy doing, from thy careful and well-meaning heart, and no worse thing ... Mall, what must I say to him?'

'Tell him he must not look to see her. She can come no more ...' I said, the tears now shaking my voice, as though it were an image in troubled water.

'Oh, Mall, dost thou mean ...?' Thomas was asking, but I was in full flight, running out of earshot, across the plain, with Ranter at my heels.

And God be my witness that saying, 'She can come no more,' I thought I had told Thomas she was dead. I meant no harm to Roland, nor did I think to cause him to suffer the pain of long-continued hope and fear. Indeed that day I had no thought of the long continuance of our suffering; for so few had died in May, and so many of those struck ill had bravely recovered, that it seemed to us all the

83

cloud was passing from us, and we would soon, soon be free.

Around us the sweet airs of May, and the breaking buds of May flowers could not but lift our spirits. And I, as I walked home, was cradling in my heart what words I meant to use to Thomas and to my father, telling them both, as I meant to do, anon, how I would be wedded at the August Wakes, as poor Emmot should have been, and how my father had best not thwart me, and talk of better men for husbands, for the world held not a better man than Thomas from edge to edge. I knew of my own knowledge now, death had brushed by so close, that life was like the flower of the field, that if you pluck it not today will not be found tomorrow. I was ready to reach for my desire, and take no heed of counsel. For would not Emmot have done better to lie with Roland first, and make a marriage later, like the poorest girls in Eyam who go to the altar swelling with sin, and full of happiness, rather than to have waited for the proper season in her virtue, and been fed on nothing but withering hope?

Let once the Plague pass from us, thought I, and if my father still refuse me, I will go to Thomas like the ewe to the ram, and father then will hasten me to church, rather than keep me from it!

But hope is cruel. When the terrors of June struck us, it was worse because we had begun to hope, to think we saw an end of it. But in June the Plague broke out suddenly in a part of the town that had scarcely been touched before – that part called the Bull Ring, where the Lydgate and Water Lane came in. The dying began again, and fast and thick carried people off. And this time, most often all who dwelt in a house wherein someone died also fell sick, and none save Marshall Howe would go in to take out the dead.

It was as though we were ashamed. Loth to crush the hope we all knew had trembled in our neighbours' hearts, as in our own. So the bell tolled no more, by which any might have counted every death. The eager gossip died; none wished to be the first to name another dead. And when the parson sent away his children at first light, riding in the saddle, the girl before and the boy behind his servant William, going over the Edge to Hazleford and bound for their uncle in Yorkshire, it was as if they had gone in secret, and certain I heard of it only from Mary Gregory, that Mary who was maidservant in the Rectory, as I have already writ.

The children were sent off for safety, Mary told us, and Catherine would have been sent too, had she consented, but she would not go unless Parson Momphesson went also. They both agreed no duty held the children. 'And they both in tears like children chidden at their lessons,' Mary said.

So the children went away, and Catherine stood in the upstairs window of the Rectory to see them go, and as they went out of sight, among the trees along the street, all screened with summer leaf, she cried aloud, 'Ah! Never shall I see them more in this life!' And her distress was so great that Mary could not calm her, but had to call the parson to come to her side.

It was as though a load of lead had been laid upon my soul to crush my spirit, when I heard the Momphesson children had been sent away. Fright and silence spread faster than even death upon the air of Eyam; none dared ask, or could bear to hear, how fared their friends and neighbours. And the empty places in the church increased faster by fear than by death or non-conformity, for nobody wished to stand close beside others.

At this time a sickness came upon me – a sickness of the stomach that went not off when I fasted for a day, but kept with me, day and night. At last I fared so ill with it, and ate so little, that my mother took me, willed-I, nilled-I, to see Goody Trickett. Mistress Trickett heard my mother out as she described my queasiness in many anxious words. Then

85

she said, very quiet, 'Old friend, herbs can do much, but they cannot take off the fear of death!'

'What, is it that?' my mother said.

'Fear sinks from the head to the stomach, very oft,' Mistress Trickett said. 'I will give her a brew of valerian to soothe her stomach, but I know a better cure if she will take it.'

'What is it?' I asked.

'Look fear boldly in the face, and vanquish it,' she said. 'I am worked off my feet, Mall. Folk batter day and night upon my door, crying out for help. I cannot make tincture and infusions fast enough, what with water to carry and plants to cull. Come you to help me, your sickness will go, I warrant it.'

She was right. With bringing clean water to her house in buckets, with taking little jugs of tinctures and teas and brews, and putting them at the doorsteps of stricken households, I soon forgot my sickness and recovered a wholesome hunger for my food. But helping Goody Trickett was no easy matter. Behind her house there was a little garden, full of physic plants, but she would have no help, nor any within sight of her, when she gathered up herbs for a medicine; she chopped and mixed all herself, and would have no help with that. Help could be given only in heating the fire, and straining off the juices from the brew.

I asked her once, meaning no harm at all, what went into a drink for Plague we were making, and she growled at me churlishly as though I had been wicked to her. But later she spoke me soft, and said, 'What I know, Mall, is all I have to live by, and I am a poor woman. I have it down from my mother and my grandmother, and she from hers before that, and many of my kindred have been in fear of being named witches for it. It is all good, what I know; I have learned no receipts to do harm to anybody, but it is secret, even from you, child.'

And by and by, finding that I knew many plants by sight

or smell, and could put a name, all unthinking, to some mess she was concocting, she sent me off, declaring that I was cured, and took as her helper Joaney Hodge's little daughter, a girl of perhaps twelve summers, pinched by hardship, who was a little simple, and could be trusted not to learn while she worked.

It seemed to me all without need or reason, such careful secrecy; Goody Trickett was not the only person in Eyam with a little knowledge of remedies, though she was esteemed by far the best. And there were Parson Momphesson's medicines now, as well as his prayers – the famous liniments from London.

I have forgot now how far June was gone when the fatal Sunday came on which our great decision was made. But June was not new, and many of those who died in June were buried already by that day. But this I do know, that it was on the very eve of that day that Francis Archdale came home. I forgot to write of his going in the right place in this my script, for his going I scarce remarked, as something not closely touching me. He had gone into Cornwall on some matter of business, bringing profit to his family, and in connection with mines. It is tin they take in Cornwall, not lead, but there are matters in which all mines are alike, and it is not an uncommon thing for there to be coming and going between Derbyshire and Cornwall, though the journey is long and troublesome. First over the Peak, and towards Liverpool, and there to take ship for some Cornish haven, the sea voyage being hazardous enough in rough weather.

But if I barely noticed the time of Francis's going, the day of his return was much remarked upon, and caused many folk to pity him and wish he had but lost more time upon the road, so that he would have been stopped from reaching Eyam and been outside and free, and not, like all the rest of us, shut in. I, for my part, could spare a thought of pity for Francis, coming home to find all at once so many losses and disasters, which we had suffered piecemeal, we whom time and too many sorrows had soon made numb. And then to find, not only home turned to a charnel house, but the door locked at his back . . .

As I have writ, we had been in a strange dullness that month of June, a liking not to know, a fearful quietness upon us; and that was broken all apart on the Sunday when Parson Momphesson told us he would close the church-yard. This he said to us in church after the end of the service, and at first we heard him, shivering in dismay, but quietly.

'My friends,' he said, 'such digging of graves, and dig-ging again hard by, and filling of Plague corpses into pits under our very feet as we come to church, and, further, the bringing of bodies through the streets, past our doors, with putrefaction already working upon them, to reach the churchyard, all this seems now to hazard the living, which neither Our Lord God, nor those who are dead, would desire us to do. From today forward, therefore, shall there be none buried in the churchyard; but in the gardens, and upon the open hillside, wherever quickest it may be done, shall we consign them to the earth, and our prayers while yet the graves are open shall be but brief . . .'

'What? Not to lie in holy ground?' cried out a woman from the back of the church, I know not who.

John Stanley, the old parson's son, made answer at once, with, 'Fie! We are as near to heaven lying beneath our own thresholds as in any ground upon earth, be it or be it not priest-blessed!'

'We shall be scattered hither and yon, and how shall he find us at the Judgement Day?' wailed Joaney Hodge.

'Tush, tush!' said Agnes Sheldon. 'Think you it could be beyond the wit of God to find thee, should he wish? But more like when he gathers the just to his bosom, he will not be seeking thee!'

'Parson,' said quiet Robert Wood, 'can we not lay each

88

man or woman a little further away from the next, but still within the churchyard?'

'My friend,' said Parson Momphesson, 'the churchyard is but a small space; and there have been laid into it already some eighty-five of thy neighbours, in this black season . . .'

It was naming the number that did it, I think. But the words were no sooner spoken than a great cry went up, in every quarter of the church, some crying, 'We are dead! All dead!' and others, 'Flee neighbours! For our lives, neighbours, flee!'

'We must forsake Eyam utterly!' cried someone in a great voice. And folk began to rush forth from the church and pour out into the churchyard, taking to their heels as though they would run away in that very instant.

Parson Momphesson went through the vestry door, and ran like the wind, so that he reached the lych-gate before any, and hollered so loud and so fiercely, crying, 'Hear me! First hear me!' like a madman, that he stemmed the rush. The folk of Eyam were penned in the churchyard like sheep in a fold, and stood like sheep flinching from the dog, swaying and on tiptoe, trembling, all together braced, as though they would run off any moment, but none would go first, and so they were held, waiting for the Judas sheep to break away, which all would follow . . . and while they hesitated, Momphesson spoke.

'My friends, the safety of all the country round about is in our keeping. If you all flee away you will take the Plague with you, far and wide. You cannot escape death by flight; many of us are already infected, though we know it not . . .' At this a groan came from the crowd, and I in the midst of the press stood so close against my neighbour I knew not if I too had groaned or no. '. . . The invisible seeds of death are hidden within your clothing, and in the bundles you would carry with you, and in your very bodies; while not saving yourselves you will bring death upon countless others as you go. Oh, will you go to God and his judgement with the guilt for deaths innumerable and suffering untold upon your souls?'

As he said this the crowd broke; Lydia Kemp took up her skirt hem in her hand and ran away, going towards the corner of the churchyard furthest from where Momphesson barred the way, with others running after her, to climb over the low wall into the street. And so, I think, the flight would have taken place, had not she, doing so, found herself suddenly facing the old parson, who had come up the street, and was standing there, looking at us all over the wall.

There was a noise of voices, telling him what was afoot, which died down abruptly, as he stared at us and said nothing.

Then Momphesson called to him across the churchyard, and across us all, 'Thomas Stanley! There is many a quarrel between thee and me, on doctrine, and on morals, and on faith. And yet I trust you, you being a man of God after your own lights, that you will stand at my side now, and help me, and tell the people that they must not go!'

Then there was a long moment while Parson Stanley drew breath . . . and Parson Stanley said, 'Stir not any from this place. What good will it do you, to flee from the will of God? Is there a place of safety, if God wills your deaths? Or any danger if he wills it not? Stay where God has appointed you to dwell, and pray without cease!'

And at that, the frenzy ebbed from us, and left us feeling weak, and much distracted. Many of the women sat down suddenly upon the grass, or leaned their weight against the trees, or the gravestones. We could hear the wind sighing on the corners of the church-tower, and going on up the Edge; we could hear the water running in the brook near by.

Then Robert Wood said, 'Parson, granted that we do not take to our heels, and scatter to the ends of the country, still every day we come and go, fetching bread and flour from

Hazleford Mill, forge-iron for the smithy, threads and needles, and fodder for cattle, much that we cannot have in Eyam, and cannot do without, unless we should starve. If the sickness clings to us invisible and may get to others in this way, might we not spread the sickness round the shire, just in our daily occasions?'

'We must bring all such traffic to a cease,' Parson Momphesson said.

'It will be very difficult to live, and full of hardship even for those who keep in health, if we do as you say, Parson,' my father said.

And Mary Heald went up to the parson, and plucked his sleeve, like a beggar woman bidding alms. 'We must go,' she said. 'Do not keep us; let us go!'

'I will not desert you,' he said. 'What help I can find, you shall have. We shall not lack the necessaries of life; I will appeal for what we need, to the Duke at Chatsworth and other worthies, and they will provide for us.'

'As have never done before, then!' cried out Marshall Howe. 'The lordly would damn their souls sooner than trouble over us!'

'But if the parson ask, for us ...' murmured Mary Gregory.

'Let him try. Much good will it do!'

'Listen to me, Marshall Howe, and all,' said Momphesson. 'We will confine ourselves utterly within the parish bounds. And so I will promise the Duke. None shall cross the parish bounds, for life or death, until the Plague has run its course and departed from us. But where the roads cross the bound, we will use the boundary-stone to leave notes of requisition for all that we have need of, and the Duke will send us those things. His messengers will leave goods early in the morning, and we not come to take them till mid-day. I will most humbly ask him for this favour; but I will tell him that unless he help us, we cannot remain within Eyam bounds, and if we cannot ...'

'From Eyam to Chatsworth is but eight mile,' said Robert Wood.

'And Plague no respecter of place and wealth,' said Father, a grim understanding in his tone.

'Parson, Parson!' called out Joaney Hodge, suddenly. 'There be no boundary-stone where the road to Hazleford goes out! And that's the way the bread comes in!'

Some of those standing nearest her harshly bade her hold her tongue, and jeeringly told her she said nothing to the point; but Parson Momphesson said, most gentle to her, 'We'll have a stone put there, hard by the roadside spring, Joan. I thank thee for bringing it to my mind.' So those who had sniggered at her were shamed by his courtesy.

'. . . And, my friends, we must all trust one another in this,' Momphesson said on. 'Who would be willing to stay, if he thought one of his neighbours might creep away in the night, and bring about the evil which he suffered to avoid? So we must swear; we will have a Bible brought out to us, and this day, before we go from hence, we will all swear that we are resolved upon: that none shall cross the parish bounds.'

'As for swearing, what says Thomas Stanley to that?' cried a voice from among us – Abel Coale I think it was.

'Aye, aye, let's hear what Parson Stanley says! How likes he this swearing? Does he not say it is but the will of God, and naught can be done to prevent it?' That was Mistress Agnes Sheldon, for all that she herself had stayed, and scorned to flee.

Then Parson Stanley stood upon the churchyard wall, where he could by all be seen, and said: 'You all know well what I have taught you in our present trouble. The Lord hath promised safety to those who trust in him. Safety he hath not promised to those who flee, having no faith, and taking thought only for their own safety. He who saves his life shall lose it; that he hath certain said to us. Some of you do believe with me that the Plague is in the immediate

92

providence of God, and fells whom he chooses only . . . and some of you perhaps believe with William Momphesson here, who has taken my place, that it goeth abroad of its own might, in seeds invisible, and that we have reason to fear the breath of the dying and the bodies of the dead. But this, certain, we do all believe. That if any man dies in Eyam who might have fled away, but who stayed for fear that in going he would infect others, then that man will gain a heavenly crown, though he be the worst sinner among us. For like Our Saviour he will have laid down his life for his friend. Who loses his life will save it, we have God's word for that. Do therefore, as you hope for heaven, as the new parson, the law's new parson, counsels you. You do no wrong to bind yourselves by oath. And I will lay my hand to this too. I will bring my Bible also, and hear oaths that in haste we may assure ourselves, and steady ourselves to the course we have set.'

We were calm then. We went through the gate, and each in turn laid a hand upon the Bible, and swore our oath. Some to Parson Momphesson's side, and some to Parson Stanley's, but we all bound ourselves alike.

Then Momphesson said, 'I must seek out all who came not to church this day, and swear them to it likewise.' He would in his haste have turned away, but Stanley said then: 'Shall I help thee, Parson Momphesson, with that task, since there are so many houses, and these new scattered huts and caves to find?'

And Momphesson said, 'I thank thee, Thomas. I would be glad of it. If thou wilt take the east parish, I will take the west.'

And so the strife between the parsons was strangely ended; and we had thrown a strong wall round ourselves, and lay imprisoned in its circuit. No troop of horse nor dungeon wall could have confined us, as we were now by our own wills confined.

*

That evening Parson Momphesson came past our door, stepping wearily down from the townhead, where he had been putting the oath to a few poor and sick; my mother called him in, and brought him a drink of elderflower tea to refresh him. He spent a while in talking to my father.

'Will the Duke help us, in good earnest, think you?' my father asked him. It was then that he told us what had happened to the Bubnell carter, how the Duke had sent a doctor to him across the stream.

'From this I learn,' said Parson Momphesson, 'that the Duke believes in precautions more than in Providence. I think he will do much in hope of keeping the country round from harm.'

'Keeping himself from harm, the while,' my father said.

'It is but common sense for him to help us,' Momphesson said.

When he had gone, 'He's not the fool he looks,' my father said.

Certainly the parson prevailed upon the Duke. The next Sunday he had a letter to read to us from the pulpit. The Duke would put all those arrangements in hand, that very day. For any exceptional or particular thing that anyone in Eyam should want, or any luxury to bring cheer in time of trouble, we should leave money steeped in vinegar upon the boundary-stones, and the Duke's servants would take it and procure our wants. But for all our necessities, for bread, for meat, for simples and medicines, he would be at his own expense to give all that we needed, in gratitude for our courage and charity for our suffering. He knew our livelihoods would be marred; he would have none suffer want. And might God keep us, and reward us with quick relief.

For this the Duke had a bushel of blessings every day from Eyam which if God heeded should have rewarded his kindness to us. Nor did he stint his charity; from that time many poor folk in Eyam ate better at his expense than ever in health they could have done at their own. Good wheaten loaves. And bacon, enough for all.

I had an aunt, living in the Lydgate, whom we saw seldom, and loved little. She was my father's sister, and had some quarrel with him that had marred matters from of old – from before I could remember. Once I inquired after the cause of it, but desisted when I saw I caused my father pain. This much I knew, that she had misliked my father's marriage to my mother, and spoken harshly about her in some way that father could not forgive, and my mother did not urge him to. My father, through hand and brain in the lead mines, and through thrift and careful adventuring, had prospered greatly, and my aunt not at all; we sent her presents of good food from time to time, but still nothing was mended. She was crabbed and bitter in her speech, and when I encountered her never let me pass without some spiteful word, so that it never crossed my mind to claim kinship with her more than needs must.

One of Eyam's many streams, called Fiddler's Brook, divided our part of the town from the lower part, and for a long time the Plague had not crossed the brook, and all who dwelt above it were in sound health. But now in the Lydgate it was raging again, bringing death every day, and soon we heard my aunt was lying sick. My poor father had spoken so strongly to my mother and me on the matter of visiting houses with the Plague in, had so rebuked us for sitting down in Sydalls' house when Emmot was struck ill, had so deplored our folly, that now he did not, for shame, say to either of us what he was going to do, but getting up very early in the morning, before even I was about, he went all alone to the Lydgate and found his sister there, dying, and made his peace with her.

And we still knew not what he had done, till one evening he pushed aside his plate at dinner, and declared he could

not eat; and my mother rising laid a hand upon his forehead, and found him burning with fever.

'Woman, it is no distemper of mine, but thy bad cooking that mars my appetite,' my father said, with spirit.
'There is no salt in this dish, and it is scorched. What man
will eat a supper that tastes of ashes?'

'Mall,' said my mother indignantly, 'is aught amiss with
the meal?'

'Mine is good,' I said.

'And mine, and all ladled from the same pot, husband!'
cried my mother.

'There, Mary, there,' my father said. 'Doubtless I do
malign thee. But help me to my bed, love, there to pay
dearly for my folly!'

And now I knew full well that he was sick indeed, hearing him use my mother's name, and admit to any folly of his
own, though still I guessed not what it was!

When we had him in his bed, and as comfortable as we
could make him, though he had begun a-shivering, he told
us very gravely that we should bring food and water to his
bedside, and going out should lock the bedroom door, and
leave the house, going to sleep with neighbours, or if need
be on the open hillside. After a week we were to return, and
if he answered not, we were to unlock the door, and send
for Marshall Howe to bury him.

'Husband, you cannot have the Plague,' my mother said.
'You have kept yourself at all times far from it, and it has not
crossed the brook. This is an ague, or such like.'

Then in a low voice he told us how he had been down to
his sister, and how he had lifted water to her lips, and
changed the foul bedding in which she was tossing about.

Thus the Plague was brought across Fiddler's Brook, into
the only part of the town that yet had not been touched, to
our harm, and to our neighbours'.

My father's instructions, that we should lock his door

and leave him to his fate, of course we disobeyed them. He was a strong man, both in body and in spirit, and he fought with death for many days. That terrible remedy, of setting a hot knife to open the tumours, my gentle mother had courage to apply, and he to ask for and endure. But to no purpose. At the end a frenzy came upon him, and he ran roaring into the street, tearing off his shirt, and going howling, almost naked, towards the lower town. Francis Archdale ran out of his house and went to restrain him, and finding that he could not, ran to fetch Robert Wood to bring him help. Only Marshall Howe could vie with Robert Wood for strength in Eyam. Robert and Francis carried my father back into the house, and up the stair to his bedchamber, and by the time they got him there the raving had ceased, and he lay quiet for his last hour.

All that hour, while I sat weeping and my mother praying, Robert and Francis together dug a grave in the garden, hard by the kitchen garth, below the apple tree, deep enough for safety, and wide enough for three. When they had done, they stopped by the casement, coming not again into the house, and told us what they had done and that we should not need to call for Marshall Howe. And I so distracted I did not thank them, by a word.

And yet some thanks were needful, for it was true friendship in them to keep us from needing Marshall Howe. He of the loud voice, and the strong frame, and the dauntless, vaunting courage had become the common gravedigger of the town. He was certain of his own safety whatsoever he did, knowing that he had caught the Plague once, and seeing that none caught it twice, save but mildly. But he had become foulmouthed and black-hearted. He laughed, when others mourned. Nor showed he any respect for the poor blotched and swollen and disfigured dead. Coming in, he brought a great iron hook, and taking up the corpse by it, would drag it down the stairs, and out along the path to a hasty hole in the garden corner, or in the field nearest behind the house. And as he laboured he swore horribly. Soon none would summon him until the last able-bodied person in the family was struck down, and in that case, seeing it was for the last survivor in each house for whom he came, he would then help himself to pewter, and bed linens, to the very food in the larder or the stool at the hearthside, or anything at all that he wanted, and would go off with it, boasting his employment to be the best paid in Eyam.

When our neighbour Unwin was reputed to be dying in a house just above ours at the head of the town, Marshall Howe rushed in, and heaved him on his back, and carried him half down the stair, when he heard a feeble voice entreating for a posset to drink. And such was the wicked man's disgust to find his neighbour living, that he threw the man down, and left him, lying on the stair just where he fell, and rushed off, crying he would be back anon! Unwin had given up hope, having lost all, being of his kin the last one living; but, he said later, his rage and his discomfort saved him, for in his anger he crawled down to the kitchen and fetched his drink himself, and thereafter felt himself better from hour to hour!

So my mother and I, together, carried my father's body down to the garden grave, and laid him quietly to rest, and covered him in, and Parson Stanley came up to bring us comfort, and pray with us a while. And for this dignity, too, I had not the wit to give neighbourly thanks!

Robert Wood, who had so helped us, lived alone but for a young nephew of some thirteen years, and a little maid-servant who was a waif and a charge upon the parish till he took her to work for him, and she shorter than his nephew by half a head. So when he felt the Plague creeping upon him, and knowing himself beyond their strength to lift or carry, he went straight away into the field behind his house, and there dug himself a grave, good and deep, and having his nephew put thick straw over the bottom of it, he tumbled himself into it, and there lay down. The two children put a blanket over him, and brought him water for a time. He lay living two days in the ground, before he died. I heard of this later, from Francis, who wept telling me.

And now I hardly know how to order this account, or which circumstances to set next. We were in such a storm of trouble, my memory stutters, and my heart shrinks from recalling it. But though I set things all awry, it could not be so disordered as we poor folk of Eyam were . . .

My father died on the twenty-sixth day of July, and we wrote that date and *William Percival* upon a wooden board, vowing him a better memento, cut in stone, some later time. And that day died four others, and five the next . . . alas, once we thought we were in dreadful danger when someone died every day; and now every day did many die together, like leaves torn off by autumn winds.

And yet, a breath of autumn wind – how welcome it would have blown! For the weather of July and August was hot, still, and heavy: not the blazing, burning heat of the summer last that had dried up all the green growing things, but a damp, grey, smothering heat, with no wind at all, not even a light air to stir the aspen leaves, or take off the terrible stenches from the town. Full easy was it to believe it was contagion of the air that brought the Plague on us, for in that weather the dissolution of the body began at a sufferer's last breath, instantly, and the stench of sickness and death reeked from the afflicted houses for days together, and never a cleansing wind to blow it off. To pass a house wherein one lay dead, and breathe the stink of it, was to feel death in the pit of one's stomach. Hours later, still one could not cough or gasp the foulness out of one's lungs.

I ran often up to the townhead, and into the open country – for the most part of the upland sheepruns was well within the parish and Liberty of Eyam – and I had to keep my sheep from the blowfly that in summer torments and endangers them. There I could drink the clean air, and the smell of grass, the hot smell of dew going off the green-sward. And there I would see Thomas from afar, and take a little joy at the sight of him, though I fled fast home again if he moved to come closer to me.

July was not out before Parson Momphesson closed the church, as well as the churchyard. In that swelter he thought we should not throng together into the airless church, and stand there within a breath of each other. And yet never more had we needed our prayers! So he locked up the church, and appointed a place to say the Divine Service in the open air. It was the Cucklett Arch he chose; I know not who showed it to him.

Eyam children all knew Cucklett Arch; had all called and whooped and romped there on summer days. There is a deep dell goes down from Eyam, from the very brink of the ledge on which the street is built to the Dale Brook, far below. The dell begins in a round hollow, which we call the Salt Pan, for its shape, and then goes between steep wooded cliffs, a narrow, but a deep cleft, down, down its way. A tiny stream runs, though barely in summer, along the bottom, and the tops of the facing cliffs break out in bare crags of grey rock, and have a number of caves in them. These were the caves that had become summer dwellings for some who were afraid to remain in their houses. Mistress Sydall was gone there, for one of many, as Emmot had dreamed she would! And because it was a lovely and a peaceful place, and very near the town, there were graves there too, dug in the soft leaf-fall of the dale bottom. Perhaps Parson Momphesson saw the Cucklett Arch for himself, visiting folk in the caves, or burying someone; but more like someone showed him. At the top of the dell, nearest the town, where the stream enters the narrow part, there is, on the western brink of the dellside, an arch of grey rock, standing clear, with an ash-tree growing hard by. There are fantastical shapes in plenty made by the rocks of the dellsides, all grey and cracked, and wind-carven; columns, and towers, and masses. But the arch is by far the strangest, for it looks as though it were the last part standing of some ruined church, though where never a church has been, and rough-hewn. And what we all knew from our childhood games was that the arch played tricks with voices; stand beneath it, and speak soft and low, and the wind at your back would carry your voice, and the rock above you throw it down, so that on the far side the dell you would be heard plain and clear, even whispering or knocking two pebbles together; though if you left the arch and cried out loudly, the listeners on the facing slope would barely catch your voice.

This place, therefore, was made our church and pulpit. On Sunday mornings we made our way into the dell, and settled upon the grass, or beneath the trees, each family together, but far spaced out from our neighbours, there to hear Parson Momphesson speak to us. And we heard the word of God, like the children of Israel in ancient time, under the sky. With each passing Sunday fewer folk came out; and all could mark and see who was missing.

That first Sunday in the Cucklett Church, Parson Momphesson spoke to us of hope. He told us God would look kindly on us, because we had had pity on our neighbours, and stayed in our places for their sake. He read to us the eighty-eighth psalm, every word. And the birds sang, and the grown lambs bleated, and the wind sighed through his speaking, but we heard him well enough:

'Oh Lord of my salvation, I have cried day and night before thee, incline thy ear unto my cry.

'I am counted with them that go down into the pit; I am as a man that hath no strength; free among the dead, like the slain that lie in the grave, whom thou rememberest no more.

'Thou hast put away mine acquaintance far from me; thou hast made me an abomination to them, I am shut up, and I cannot come forth.

101

'*Shall thy lovingkindness be declared in the grave? Or thy faithfulness in destruction?*

'*But unto thee have I cried, Oh Lord, and in the morning shall my prayer prevent thee.*

'*I am afflicted and ready to die, from my youth up; While I suffer thy terrors I am distracted, Thy fierce wrath goeth over me, thy terrors have cut me off.*

'*Lover and friend hast thou put from me, and my acquaintance into darkness!*

'These words were written long ago,' Parson Momphesson told us, 'that seem as they were written in special for us now of Eyam. In trouble and affliction, the psalmist said, "But unto thee I have cried, Lord, and in the morning shall my prayer prevent thee." So put he his trust in prayer, and yet this was before the coming of Jesus, our sweet Saviour, whose mercy we may trust, for eternal life. Shall not our prayer sooner prevent the Lord's anger, that we make in the name of his Son?'

And all the while he spoke thus, the birds sang on, as though there were no trouble in the world at all.

Coming up from the dell, climbing the slope back into Eyam, we kept a safe distance from all but Agnes Sheldon, she of the providential ducks, but she stepped alongside my mother and me and began to rail upon the new parson. 'For making us worship in a field like heathen folk, and all for shameful fear, as though we had bad consciences! What a deal of secret wickedness there has been in Eyam, neighbour!' said she. 'Some have felt the Lord's anger that I, for one, knew well were given to swearing or drinking, or going behind the cowsheds with sluttish wenches, or turning off poor folk that came for alms with nothing in their pinny pockets, or their jug, while plenty was to spare within the pantry, leave alone those who steal thimbles, or take eggs . . .' She paused, needs must, for breath. 'But who would have thought your husband, neighbour, who always thought himself so fine, and looked you in the eyes

102

like an honest goodman ever, was like an apple rotten out of sight, and ripe for the Lord's punishment? He and many another I always thought well of . . .'

My mother stopped in her tracks. I thought she would have blasted Mistress Sheldon with some fierce bastanado of reply; but she turned sudden away, saying nothing.

'Humph! humph!' said Agnes Sheldon, as astounded as I at mother's silence I think, and took herself off.

When we were safe within doors, I said, 'Was there no answer, mother, to a speech as vile as that?'

'Alas, Mall,' my mother said, sinking into the chair by the fire-corner, 'I sudden remembered your father saying he would trust not God for safety in a mine . . . he talked often like an unbeliever, Mall. Perhaps she hath the right of it . . .' I left her crying while I made a brew of chamomile tea to comfort her withal. I would have nettle-whipped Agnes Sheldon from one end to the other of Eyam town had I been able, but I had to content myself with wishing the Lord might find as sharp an eye for her unkindness as she for others' faults; which thought I soon unwished, and sore repented. We had no need to wish trouble down on any head in Eyam!

My mother was in a strange condition after my father died. She brought me in mind of a bird I found once, a young thrush that a cat had caught, that had lost all its tail-feathers. It was found not to be otherwise hurt, when we chased off the cat, and rescued it in the barn. It chirped and hopped, and flapped its wings, and made to fly – but in flying it tumbled over and fell down, and so, baffled, hopped and chirped, and flew and fell, over and over till its strength was spent.

Thus would my mother, rising early, begin upon some task, some washing or cooking, or sweeping of hearth or floor . . . and then all sudden stop, and look amazed, as though she knew not why she did it, and at once sit down, leaving all in mid-way. 'I am well enough,' she would say.

'Take no care. I will rise presently, and set to.' And so she would again, beginning on another thing, and soon abruptly leaving it. And ever upon her face the look of one who has lost the way, or quite forgot some needful thing.

Strangely, when Parson Stanley came to talk to her of the Lord's will, which ever till then she had heard gladly, she turned away her face, and answered him very little, joining to his prayer not so much as 'Amen'. But then Parson Momphesson came in, and began to talk to her a tittle-tattle, of some fine device he had seen used in Nottingham – to wit, a 'water-ball', this being a glass globe filled up with water, and set in a window, or before a candle – this, he said, greatly increased the force of the light, so that the lace-makers could work after daylight faded. A wonderful ingenuity, he said. And he was having a glass-blower make a dozen globes for his Catherine to have good light by for her reading and her sewing; and should they all come unbroken, right gladly would he give one to my mother that she too might profit by it ... and at this my mother perked up, and listened, and got out of her chair, and busied herself with bringing a drink for the parson, and seemed to welcome the proffered gift of a water-ball, and had even a smile upon her face.

Such run-a-gate talk was flowing free, when sudden the parson said that it were as well to burn the bed my father died in, and carefully clean the house, and he would give a receipt for the best fashion of doing it...

'Why as to that, good Parson,' said my mother, sweetly smiling, 'I care not a pin whether I live or die.'

'But your sweet child, Mistress. For your daughter's sake, you must do as if you cared.'

My mother tipped her head to one side, as though she had truly been the bird I likened her to. 'I'll get a cleansing bunch from Goody Trickett, and scrub the floors there-with,' she said, 'if it will do Mall any good at all.'

'Goody Trickett means well enough,' said he. 'But she is

but a prating quacksalver, when the truth is known. My Lord Duke hath sent me the newest book of physic herbs, got up from London, newly printed, wherein it is said that water of rue will kill fleas, sprinkled freely about, and drive out the seeds of Plague, where they lie unseen. And is it not rue growing right beside your door?'

'No, no!' my mother said, 'that is but herbygrass that I grew for my own mother's backache, many years agone.'

'Herbygrass?' he said, laughing. 'I have never heard it called that. Herb-of-grace, it is sometimes called. Make use of it, Mistress Percival, and God be with you.'

So he took his leave, and my mother got up, and boiled a bunch of rue in a bucket, and sprinkled and washed with it everywhere. Then she went up to bed and slept the day out, leaving the bucket of acrid green stinking in the middle of the floor.

I was surprised at my mother, though glad enough she should seem more cheerful, even if I could not tell why. The next day Mary Gregory came to her, sent by her mistress, Catherine Momphesson, saying that the parson had seen in our house a pair of stockings hung by the fire to dry, knitted after a very pretty pattern, and Catherine asked my mother to step down to the Rectory and show her the pattern as she was to make a pair of stockings for her little daughter, to send as a present when it would be safe to do so.

My mother brushed her hair and put on a clean pinafore, and went off with Mary, and was gone most of the day. I free, therefore, ran off to my sheep, and to glimpsing Thomas.

Thomas himself drove me home, he coming too close, and calling to me with such a longing in his voice I was afraid I would rush into his arms. He knew not that the Plague was come now in my very house, and I not now just perhaps, but very certainly a danger to him. I was tired, and not so nimble as before, and I was hard put to it to flee fast home again, and had a stitch in my side, so I stopped by Sheldons' pond, and leaned upon a gatepost to recover myself. Whereupon Agnes Sheldon came out to me, and asked me if I would have a cup of water, and I thanked her and said yea. And while I was drinking from her cup she began again upon her bitter talking. There were some she knew that supposed themselves safe enough, when the Lord was but holding back his hand the better to strike.

'Why, whoever do you mean, Mistress Sheldon?' said I, crossly, being sure she meant me.

'What of that whore who brought it all upon us?' said Agnes. 'Shall she go unscathed? Foolishness and vanity!'

And when I still, as I suppose, looked blankly at her, she went on, 'All for a dress, Mall! All for the sinful pleasure of arraying the corrupt body in silks cut in heathen outlandish fashion! All for the evil joy of exciting lust in every eye! Surely she will not much longer walk free, as I pray God she will not!'

At that I cast her cup from me, and ran away, holding my hands against my ears. I met with my mother on the threshold, she just coming home from the Rectory, and we went in together, and began getting ourselves a supper.

'Mother, is Agnes Sheldon any kind of witch, and can she do any harm?' I asked her.

'Never that I heard, Mall. She is just a proud woman with a waspish tongue . . . why ask you?'

I told her the words I had had from Mistress Sheldon, and my mother sat down very sudden in her chair, and said, 'God keep the good lady! But as we were sitting with the stockings all but knit up, the parson came in, and Catherine, getting up, opened a casement, and then said she, "William, I would like to walk out, and take the air. How sweet it smells!" And he said, "Doth it, Catherine?" and went to the window himself; and then he looked at me, and so took her arm in his, and went out across the garden with her . . . I am troubled for her, Mall.'

'For that she would walk?'

'Why, when she opened the window, I marked nothing!'

'Mother,' I said, eager to comfort her. 'Does not God's open air always smell sweet, when windows are cast wide?'

'I marked it not,' my mother said, stubbornly. 'Mall, when we are done with supper, come with me, we will go and pray for her.'

'The church is shut up, mother, and there is nowhere better to pray than here.'

'We will pray by the old cross in the churchyard, Mall, where folk of Eyam gathered to their prayers before ever there was a church here.'

I was willing to humour her in this, or in anything as long as it seemed to cheer her; and heavy though her spirits were, fretting for another's sake, it was better than too much fretting and mourning her own sorrow.

The weather was still sultry, a heaviness and a sweat in the air, as it had been weeks past. Yet as we walked we found a smoke of fires in the street. Folk were bringing kindling and building huge fires, beside the stocks, and at the churchyard gate, and further down in the Bull Ring, and to judge by the smoky dirt smudge on the sky, perhaps still more. As we walked, neighbours told us, frenzied in their manner of speaking, that someone had said in London they lit fires in the street to purify the air, and we should try that too . . .

In vain. As my mother and I begged the Lord to have done with his anger, and to forgive us poor women such frailties as liking dresses and ribbands . . . the skies opened, and there came down a flood of rain upon us that wet us to the skin, and straight put out the fires! We walked home past hissing piles of quenched kindling, and the charred half-burned twigs washed in the gutter past our feet and smudged black our soaking shoes and hems.

For just one day next, there was a washed coolness in the

107

air of Eyam. Then came the sunless warmth again, and the damp ground perspired into the air, and all was clammy.

Praying for Catherine Momphesson, my mother had asked the Lord's mercy for her because she had not fled away from Eyam, but kept faithful at her husband's side. We both prayed every day for every soul in Eyam, reminding the Lord that we might have fled, and saved ourselves at hazard of all the country round, but instead had kept our places. I think that each and every one of us, whatever sins were in our secret hearts, had yet some pride, felt yet some claim on God's mercy, for heeding what the parsons said, and staying put.

Then one morning very early, as August went on, a woman who lived at Orchard Bank got up, and went away, across the parish bounds and to Tideswell. She was Aliss Frith, a simple poor woman, a spinster, something older than I. She lived in a row of cottages upon Orchard Bank, that rises alongside the street in the upper town and has gardens going back towards Bradshaw Hall. She had a sister living in Buxton, and as day after day folk sickened and died all round her, she lost courage and vowed to save herself, let the devil take the rest of the world! She put her few things together in a kerchief and crept away, going to Tideswell market, where she thought many would be bound, and she could step through the crowds, and leave to Buxton along with many others, and so escape unremarked. Her sister, as she trusted, would shelter her.

But on the Tideswell road she met a watchman set, who challenged her. And three others with stout sticks came up and stood across the road.

'Where are you from?' they asked.

'Why do you ask?' said she.

'None from Eyam pass this way,' they told her. 'Where are you from?'

'From Orchard Bank,' she said.

'Where is that?' the watchman asked.

'Why, verily, 'tis in the land of the living!' she said, as though she would joke with them, and they laughed and stood aside, and she went on her way. But her luck did not hold; in the throng at Tideswell market, through which she went light of heart, glad to be in a crowd again and with a bustle around her, and all of folk in good health and without fear, she saw sudden a man who was known to her, and he in the same moment saw her. He cried out at once, 'A woman from Eyam!' The whole crowd set up a howling and shouting, 'The Plague! The Plague! A woman from Eyam!' and whichever way she turned they shrank from her, and then ran after her, screaming and throwing things, pelting her first with fruit and turnips from the stalls, and then, as they blocked her way any way but back on the Eyam road, and as she ran weeping that way, and out of reach of the market, they picked up stones and pelted her with those. As far as the watchmen on the road they chased her, throwing stones. And then the watchmen with their cudgels came at her back right to the parish bound. So she came weeping home again, all bruised and bleeding, and the neighbouring wives found her fainting in the road for weariness and soreness, and took her within and tended her.

This Aliss was much afraid that the parsons, either one of them or the other, would rebuke and scold her, and name her for a breaker of oaths, and shame her in front of others; and yet none, as far as I heard, had the heart to reproach her, for the heaviness her story brought us. We had thought ourselves, till then, as close to saints, who willingly remained in Eyam for others' sake; now we knew ourselves as prisoners, caged in whether we would or no. We had thought the people round about would have regarded us with gratitude; it seemed now they looked on us as a shepherd on a wolf, setting guards to watch against us, ready to pelt and pummel us on sight. A thought to sink our hearts, that were so sorely laden already.

*

I have written already that whereas we had once been in mortal fear because some one of us died each day, it came about that so many would die upon a single day, we counted that day kind on which only one person perished! And whereas we had once fallen praying, for fear that there might not be a family in Eyam that did not lose one of its members, yet now we saw commonly whole families that perished all together, to the last one.

There was a place called Shepherd's Flat, on the edge of Eyam but within the parish bound, on the upland pastures; a cluster of cottages where dwelt two families, Kemps and Mortins, keeping flocks, and a few hens, and two cows, and killing hares and rabbits for the pot, and growing a patch of beans. Their sheep and ours had often to be sorted by our dogs, and at shearing we had always worked together with them, and shared the labour, and the ale, and the clip-supper afterwards. Good honest folk. The Kemp children played at tag-and-seek with children from Eyam town that August, and came home sickening, to their mother's frantic grief, she being a widow. Mother and children of the Kemps all died, and the Mortin father, Matthew, out of neighbourly charity, buried them. Within a day his own child, Sarah, aged but two, died sleeping, and he dug a grave for her by his house gable-end, and laid her there. Margaret his wife was carrying a child and near her time when she too sickened. And finding none would set foot in his house to help his wife, Matthew helped forth his child himself, while his son Robert, but of three years old, had perforce to be locked in a chamber near by, he now having the fever and having not wit enough at his tender age to keep in bed. The child screamed all the time his brother was being born, to his father's grief. And this was not yet bad enough, for before the week was out, Matthew Mortin laid his son Robert also, and his wife, and his son new born, in the grave by the gable-end, and dwelt at Shepherd's Flat alone, with but his greyhound and his cows for company. And so plentifully had the hares and rabbits flourished while men so declined, there being none to hunt and trap and take them, that the uplands were all overrun with small game, and Mortin's hound could bring him meat within a few short minutes, any time of day. So he sat solitary, stirring not out, and the dog brought him victuals, and he milked his cows for them both.

I went ever more seldom up to the sheepruns now, but there was a day when I went, and found one of Mortin's sheep grazing with some of mine and some of Thomas's. The poor beast was torn about the shoulder, and soaked in clotted blood, as though a wild dog had savaged it. And that not unlikely, for many a dead man's dog went unfed in Eyam to scavenge for itself that time. But I wondered that it seemed to have got no help, for Mortin was a good hand with the flocks, and a careful man and watchful, who had more than once saved lamb of mine from eagle, and should have saved his own. I went up a hillock not far from Shepherd's Flat, and saw not a soul moving, though I lingered, waiting for someone I might hail. At last I whistled Ranter to drive the beast down into the yard beside the house. The poor ewe bleated piteously, making hard weather of going so far, yet still no one came out. And I, full of fear, went no closer.

Indeed, as I stood there, Thomas's dogs came fawning joyfully at my feet, and I, startled, looking round found him hard by, and coming fast towards me. I ran off, running along the road to Eyam, and then once within the town I climbed the track by Bradshaw Hall, and began to mount the steep slope upwards to Eyam Edge, meaning to gain the ridge and go out that way, towards Bretton, and so a long way round unto my sheep again. It is a hard climb up the Edge, and I had not gone far before Thomas appeared before me, descending fast, having forestalled me. So I turned back, and took no heed, though he called my name after me enough to tear heart out of ribcage. Back then

111

within the town traipsed I, and down the Cussy Dell, below the Cucklett Church, its rocky arch, and through the wood's solitariness and coolness, a most fair, flowery path, well shaded, right to the dell foot, where it opens to the Middleton road, and the Dale Brook. The brook is the parish bound, so keeping to the Eyam bank I followed the brook along, meaning to reach the upland by Foolow way; and there again Thomas lay in wait for me. He hid himself upon a rocky crag, overlooking the track, and overhung with boughs, and I should have passed perilously close by him had not Ranter found him out, with standing on his back-legs, upright, his front paws upon the cragside, and his tail wagging, and he barking in his witless joy at meeting of a friend.

So fled I home the third time, and for weariness set forth no more. I had hope that when Thomas was done foolchasing after me he might return and find the injured sheep, and kill it, for nothing else was to be done for it. But later I stepped down, and knocked on Parson Stanley's door, and asked him if he knew of aught amiss at Shepherd's Flat, and from him I heard what I have just set down.

The folk at Shepherd's Flat were not the only entire families to be swept away wholesale, dust in the storm of the pestilence. As grisly was the fate of those who lived at Riley. There were Talbots there, blacksmiths and farriers, and their house was set hard by the Sheffield road, a quarter mile or so outside the town, to the east, where they might catch custom from folk going by. It was an airy spot on high ground, and should have been a wholesome place. Bridget and Mary, Talbot's daughters, were full fair young women, famous for their bloom. And how the Plague reached out to them I do not know, but both girls died, and on the same day. And two days after, Ann, their sister, died, still a child, and then eleven days and Catherine Talbot their mother died, and shortly after father and two sons died also, and not a soul alive from that large and prosperous family, save for one son who was away from Eyam the day we closed the parish bounds, and so could not come home.

John Hancock buried the last Talbot to die. Hancocks lived but a few yards off, and shared a small garden plot with Talbots, for their pot-greens. And when Hancocks began to die there were already none left well enough within the house except for Mistress Hancock, the mother, but all the rest lay sick. With her own hands, therefore, she dug graves and buried them. Her daughter Elizabeth she buried on the open hillside, outside the house and garth, what distance she had strength to drag her body, taking her by a towel knotted round her feet; and later on that same day, her son John. It was the third day of August. On the morning of the seventh of August she had to bury three – her sons Oner and William and her husband John, who had quit this world within minutes of each other in the night. And yet not done; on the ninth Alice her daughter was to drag out and cover over, and on the tenth her daughter Ann. And having thus interred as best she could every living soul of her kindred except herself, she fled unnoticed, oath or no oath, across the bounds and out of Eyam, and went, they say, to her son apprenticed far away and has come back no more. We never heard that she took the sickness with her. It must be she was in health when she fled. Poor woman, I cannot blame her.

From the top houses of Middleton there is a prospect across to Riley, over the top of the woods, to the open ground the other side of the Dale. And morning after morning, much later Roland told me, the folk of Middleton could watch with horror poor Mistress Hancock dragging out her dead, and digging them in. Greatly they pitied us, and heartfelt were their prayers for the prisoners in Eyam, but more greatly yet they feared to share our fate. And every man and wench and boy and dog in Middleton was set to watch Roland, and keep him from coming Eyam way but a

113

step, though he, poor Roland, had mistook my message to Thomas; or rather one day he took 'She will come no more' as meaning Emmot was dead, and the next he taught himself to think it meant but that she was kept from coming to him, as he from going to her . . .

Not everyone could be watched as Roland was. Aliss Heald, who had been married down to Curbar at the last Wakes, came by night to see her mother – some day in July I think it should have been. She found her mother dying, and in terror crept home again. Poor girl, she took the sickness with her, and died in Curbar three days afterwards. They of Curbar were in great perturbation but none of them took sick from her, not even the poor woman they paid to nurse her, nor the gravedigger who buried the putrid corpse.

There was fear and awe in all the country round, as I was told. From this and that prospect, sight could be seen of Eyam, her houses, and her plague-huts, and outlying cottages. And when we dug graves, outsiders spied us doing it, or saw the fresh-turned brown earth on the hillside turf. And another thing signalled our woes abroad; the Duke sent still the bread and bacon and beer to us in ample quantity, soon more by far than the living could eat up. So we took less, and left some lying at the boundary-stones. Still less was brought to us, and we took less by the day. And the sight of the spare loaves lying struck chill into the hearts of the Duke's servants.

We had a horror of Marshall Howe, as I have set down, when I wrote that we had Francis Archdale and Robert Wood to thank for needing him not when my father died. But it was not for dislike of roughness or of swearing that poor Mistress Hancock struggled to bury her dead all unaided; Marshall Howe's evil speech did little harm really, nor yet his taking things from empty houses. I think he blustered so to keep his courage high; certain no one could have done his task, without they hardened their heart

114

exceedingly against others' sorrows. If we had not thought of this, nor well esteemed him for his services, yet when his help failed us before our need ceased, the lack of him taught us to esteem him better! It was thinking himself secure, from having had the Plague and recovered from it, that supported that rough man's hardihood. Alas, when in late August Joan his wife fell ill, and swelled up in her neck and armpit, and after much suffering died, Marshall Howe thought he had brought the sickness unto her about his person from his fearful task, and bitterly repented him.

With tears and gentleness he bore her out of doors, unto the meadow by the townhead, and with not a single blasphemy he laid her in the ground below a tree, and filled the grave with wild flowers from the hedge before he earthed her in. Then going home he found his son William lying fevered and discoloured upon the floor. Four days later William Howe too was buried. Then Marshall Howe sat in his house alone, lamenting his foolishness, and he would come forth no more, nor dig another grave for anyone, but sat like a lost-wit, broken in hope and strength.

So day by day we went from bad to worse, and then to worser yet. And day by day the worst we feared befell us, and the least hope we had was spoiled.

My mother, for example of it, had feared for Catherine Momphesson, only for that the lady had found the air of evening scented sweet, and wished to walk in it. But the very next day we heard that Catherine Momphesson lay sick and the swellings were on her body. She had but a short illness, having small strength to pit against the raging of the disease, she having consumption already as we had guessed. She besought her husband to come not near her, for his safety, but he in great grief and unquietness yet comforted himself that he should do all he could for her. When the fever and delirium possessed her, yet still she cried upon the name of her Saviour. When she would not drink the cordials he made for her out of his London book, he persuaded her to it, by speaking of her children, and asking her to sup for their sake. At last the calm came, and she lay quiet and obedient, and like, it seemed to him, to recover; and he sat and read to her the prayers for the sick, and the catechism, as he would do for any of his parishioners.

All this while Mary sat upon the stairs, listening at the chamber door, in case she would be called for some thing, and readier to lose her own life – though she never for an hour sickened – than to lose her young mistress. Some time the parson went to sleep a while, he at the limit of his strength for watching, and coming and going from one sickbed to another. Catherine called Mary to her, and asked her forgiveness for having given her a cross word, Mary not being able to remember any such at all. Then, later, Catherine would pray, and her husband came to her again. There by the light of tapers he read the prayers to her, and she said low, 'Amen'. And then he came to an end, and she answered not.

'My dear,' he said soft, 'dost thou hear?'

'Yes!' she said, starting up a little, and that the last word that she spoke, for as she moved she died.

They say at midnight, while Mary wailed and cried, Thomas Stanley rose up, and crossed the street, and went into the Rectory, wherein he had not set foot since Saint Bartholomew's Day four years before, and going in to William Momphesson as though they had been brothers, he prayed with him.

They would have made exception for her, to lay her in the churchyard, and in holy ground, but if they could find someone to dig the grave for her decent and deep. Marshall Howe would not; and there were so few left now in health. Weakness and fear, the long aftermowth of the sickness in those recovered, the sights and smells of horrors, and nights sleepless with fear or nursing, had sapped us all to

116

the dregs. And six feet down is far to dig, in Eyam's hard hillside stony ground. Our parsons both were still in health; but with coming and going day and night, breathing ever the air of deathbeds, sleeping never more than an hour but someone woke them and brought them to another charnel scene, writing wills for each man in turn all round the town, and shortly undertaking to perform them, they were faint and worn. Together they prayed God to send them a gravedigger; and either by God's doing or by mine their prayer was answered.

In this way. The day that Catherine Momphesson fell ill, my mother was stricken also. She seemed not ill; but at her elbow there came a swelling that stiffened her arm, and she said she could not see, for the angel's wings that beat across the room. Even my face, she said, was all obscured by golden feathers. I took her to her bed, with what fear in my heart may be imagined. My mother was a strong and sturdy woman, well used to working the day long. And she was not far advanced in age. I think she had the Plague but mildly, compared to many. By rights she should have had good prospect of recovery. But she did not want to live. She fought death not at all, but meekly waited for its victory. So, finely balanced, life and death each close at hand disputed over her. While I left not her side.

My sheep were in God's hands, or Thomas's; for many days I went not up to them, but simply sat indoors, doing what I could for my mother. And scarcely had I leisure to think of Thomas, what he would think, seeing me not, since the day he drove me three times hasting home. But one night I rose from my chair and went to close the casement, for my mother was shivering in her sleep, and the room had become chilled with the night air. There was a bright moon shining, and by its ghostlight I saw Thomas, standing by the garden wall and turning his face towards the window where I stood. I ran down, and bolted the door against him. And by and by, as I stood with my candle in

117

my hand, looking upon the latch, I saw it tried from the other side, softly and quietly.

I knew I could not keep him from me while I lived. I was afraid, to heartbreak, for his sake.

At daybreak, therefore, I went to seek out Francis, and I asked him to help me. 'Go up the hill, to within call of Thomas,' I asked him, 'and say to him that I am dead. Tell him to come no more, therefore.'

Francis much misliked it. 'This is a lie, Mall,' he said, with a troubled look. 'No good can come of it.'

'Francis, we have known each other from the cradle,' I said, 'and I have none to ask save you. As you love me, do this for me. The lie be upon my conscience, not on yours.'

'Yet find another messenger, Mall, I entreat you,' he said. 'Thomas will more readily believe another than me.'

'Why should he so?' I asked, bewildered. 'I had not thought you would refuse me, Francis!'

'Very well,' he said, turning his face away from me. 'I will do it. This day, Mall, it is done.'

Francis went up the track nearly to Shepherd's Flat. He stood upon a hillock, cupped his hands, and called for Thomas into the four winds. Soon Thomas came, hieing hard towards him with his dogs at his heels, and called to Francis, 'What news from Eyam, friend?'

'The Lord chastises us, to the limits of his anger,' Francis said. 'We have not so much as strength among the living to bury the dead. Ask me not how she fares, Thomas. Thy Mall is dead!'

And mistrusting his own courage for telling lies under question, Francis took to his heels at that, and hied fast home again. He stopped at my door, to tell me it was done.

'How did he look, at this?' I asked, wistfully. I fain would have heard that he laid his face in his hands and wept . . .

'I did not stop to see,' Francis told me.

*

118

Thomas told me, he stood upon the bare hills under the steep light of rising day. Whichever way he looked, remembrance smote him. He saw a tree whereunder we had sat, he and I together, to have a shade. He saw a stream that I had leaned down to, to drink from. He saw my sheep with his sheep, and Ranter running with Bess and Noll. By rainlight and by snowlight he saw me coming, and he saw the blood to my elbow in a cavern of drift, and I but a slip of child. He thought how once a stranger had come unto him, and spoken to him of inner light. He, Thomas, had laughed and declared the outer light upon the hills was light enough; and the stranger had answered that a man must have the inner light to see the outer by. And now, now, Thomas told me, inner darkness overwhelmed his soul. He looked on the land without hope, and saw it not, even as the stranger had said.

Then he walked northwards, and climbed up Eyam Edge, and so along the brink of the Edge, until the town lay all below him in his view. He saw the long street winding far below, set about with houses and gardens. He saw the church tower rise square among the trees, and in the dells beyond the town he saw the tops of trees that brimmed the clefts in the land with boughs and leaves. He saw a scatter of huts where folk dwelt like beggars under wattles, on the heath. And in the light of his darkness, he saw what he would do.

Then he plunged over the scarp, and lurched like the land, downwards, running, arms spread like a bird starting into flight, across the steep grassy slopes, down, down, till trees and church tower top were level with his gaze, and then rose up over his head, high above him, the church tower growing and growing, until he leapt the churchyard wall, and stood at the church door, and the tower was still, tall above him, and there he stopped.

He had been seen coming. Folk all bewildered walked into the street, and stood to see him down. He came from the churchyard to the street, to face many pairs of eyes. Folk thronged not close together, nor all surged to come near him, but stood piecemeal staring at him like oxen in a field.

And here came both the parsons, side by side, from the Rectory door.

'Thomas, what do you here?' demanded Stanley. 'Know you not that once here you cannot depart from us? What have you done, coming headlong down?'

'I have lost all hope of joy in this world,' Thomas said. 'And I am come to stand full in the whirlwind, that it may carry me sooner to the next. No light is left for me to see by, any other way.'

'But what do you mean, son? What do you mean?' said Stanley, in amaze.

I had risen that morning early, not having left the house for many days, and gone out, leaving my mother sleeping. The fever afflicted her sorely; and though I knew well there was no simple for the Plague, yet Goody Trickett could pluck a plant to cool a fever, and I thought could I but cool my mother's burning limbs, her strength might rally yet against the disease. So on a fine fair morn I went forth on my errand.

Goody Trickett's door was standing wide. Her chickens pecked across the kitchen floor, and a rat lay dead in the ashes of the cold hearth. I climbed the stair, dreading what I might find. The upper room was all disordered, and the rats ran upon the rumpled bed. I looked out through the casement where I stood, and saw the new-turned hump of earth in the gardenside. There would no more help be found from Goody Trickett. I spared no thought for her, being full of care elsewhere. 'Had she but taught me,' I thought, 'what harm would my knowing of her secrets do her now?' Going downstairs I looked around, and tried hard to remember. Had she a book of lore hid somewhere? Not like; all was in her head. Had she not told Bridget and

Eliza she could not read or write? I looked at the bunches of herbs hanging up drying on the lintel of the fireplace, and crumpled a pinch within my fingers. I knew it not by shape or odour.

Then going to the garden door, I looked out at her beds of simples. Some things I knew the name and use of well enough, and of many more I knew neither. And well I understood her having said that some of her brave brews were poison, deadly to those who had not the malady they were sovereign to. Ratbane and antbane, and a death for foxes she had been used to make for folk, as well as physic . . . and as I looked, of a sudden I saw a patch of little bushes all bare to the twigs – a plant of which she had had many, some three dozen rows, and not a leaf left on any a one! This surely must be what she used for plague-fever; of every other plant plenty remaining, and this one only being all consumed! But how was I to know what plant it was?

Earnestly I studied it. A little low bush, thick branching. Some stems brown, some green and soft – a thing then that put forth growth each year, but survived the winter, the last season's growth hardening with the cold. I broke a naked sprig of it, some two inches long, and rubbed it hard upon my palm, and laid my nose to it . . . I wondered if some small trace of its virtue might lie in the stem, and if I could boil it . . . I thought it would be something rare and strange, and hard to find even if well known to the searcher . . .

Only the faintest fragrance remained in the dry twig, a smell that lasted but one breath upon my skin – but sage! it was *sage*! Sage that grew by every gate in Eyam! And we too had two or three bushes of it; mother should have a tea of it instantly!

So with a tickle of hope, I held my hems and ran, ran full tilt towards home. And coming round the corner into the street by the church, I came to Thomas, face to face.

*

121

'What, Mouse, and art thou living? I am come to dig thy grave!' he said.

'Thomas, I sent thee tidings that should have kept thee hence for ever!' I cried.

And in our stammering words, our neighbours soon understood what had befallen.

'The poor doves . . . poor souls . . . and now he must bide, come what . . .' I heard murmured from bystanders.

'It is true, friend, we cannot let thee now depart,' said Parson Momphesson.

'Fear me not,' said Thomas, and his voice was steady and glad. 'I will not flee, any more than other folk have done that dwell in Eyam. I thought, "If she be dead, then nothing in the world is there worse to fear, and my own death is swiftly to be sought for"; and I find if she lives and loves me still, it is that which shall make me fear nothing. And, Mall, right sorry am I that I came not sooner to this knowledge. What a weary time we have spent, far from each other! To be parted from each other while we live, that at least, love, we need fear no more!'

Momphesson stood hard by, with tears upon his face that flowed silently. Then, 'Friend,' he said, 'friend Thomas, there is no grave to dig for thy love, certainly; wilt thou for pity dig a grave for mine?'

'A spade,' said Thomas, 'and I am the man for that. Did I forget to say I am come to be your gravedigger? And my life be in the Lord's hands.'

So I left him at work, and took myself home to make a brew of sage and give my mother.

That evening Thomas came home to me. He brought the pulse of life with him to our sad empty rooms, he all untouched by sickness, with his candid and unhaunted eyes, his heart laden not with remembered horrors, burdened not with loss, his smile easy, and his strength at a young man's fullness. He brought me comfort, and he brought me joy, for all the fear and grief around me. But my mother took his coming most strangely, in that it made her readier to die. I had understood full well that it was her will to conquer the sickness and rise up again that flagged in her heart, rather than her body that was overcome. When I brought her the brew of sage I spoke to her.

'Mother,' I said, 'do not leave me. I am but a poor foolish wench, with little wisdom, and I am not ready to be without father and mother in this hard world. That stocking stitch you know you never yet taught me, nor have you showed me how to make apple comfits – and how oft have you said I wash a floor but ill!'

Then, 'Tush, child,' she said. 'You will do very well. I have no fear for thee, Mall. Look in your father's reckoning books; you will find yourself well provided for. Marry your Thomas, presently. You will do well.'

I took her hand then, and said, 'Mother, do not leave me! Stay with thy poor Mall . . .'

'Child, do not ask it,' she said, very soft. 'Let me go.'

So I unclasped her hand, and sat by a while. And she seeming then to be falling asleep, I left her.

An hour later Thomas, going in to see how she fared, found her dead.

We buried her by my father, in the grave made ready by the pear-tree behind the house. Thomas Stanley came and said funeral prayers. When he had done he came within the house, and looked sternly upon us.

'Will Thomas come to my house this night, and there abide, Mall? Or will he take thee now to wife, and shall I find a witness, and call upon Parson Momphesson?'

'Is this a time to think of wedding?' I said.

'It is a time you have need of comfort, Mall. But a bad time to have a sin upon your soul, which may go to the Lord any day, any hour. You cannot live alone with Thomas under one roof, unless he be your husband.'

'I cannot think of this now,' I said.

123

'Come then, Thomas, and I will find thee bed and board,' said Parson Stanley, and opened the door, and stood at it, for Thomas to go out with him. So I saw I would be all alone in the empty house.

'Don't go, Thomas,' I said, in a small voice.

I barely minded what next befell. But I do remember Parson Momphesson, haggard and grave, putting question to me, beside the cold house-hearth, would I take Thomas better or worse, richer or poorer, until death...

They had found Francis to be the second witness, after Parson Stanley. Poor Francis, he looked strange, and brought a suffering face to the task.

'Francis, what ails thee?' I said, all out of order, when all looked to me to say yes, or amen, or suchlike.

'Do not mind me, Mall,' Francis said, looking even more strangely on me. 'Give answer to the parson, girl, see where Thomas waits.'

'Yes,' I said then. 'Yes.'

'You must say, "I will," child,' said Parson Momphesson to me, in a most gentle tone.

'I will,' I said, obedient to them all. Thomas had from somewhere – from Parson Stanley as I think – a ring, that was put upon my finger. And I stood stupid, rooted to the spot, saying nothing after I said, 'I will.'

Parson Momphesson told Thomas he must take out and burn the bed in which my mother died, and all her clothing too, and wash with rue-water ... Francis told Thomas he must mind and keep the dogs within doors, which word at that time I understood not.

And then they departed all, and left us together, man and wife.

I have heard both parsons say there is no joy in this world, and they are wrong, are wrong! Where man and maid are wedded to their own good liking, there is joy. And I have heard Parson Stanley say such earthly joy is but a trick, a feigning and all the devil's making, to lead poor souls astray. And by that I know it is a joy he hath not tasted, for none who in their own flesh knew it could mistake it so. It is from God; I think it is a foretaste of the rapture of the saints, given to be a beacon to us unto heaven, to whet our longing for our immortality.

There were seventy-six of my fellow villagers carried to the grave in the month of August alone, out of so shrunk and diminished a number, and September came on, and still every day people died. But I grieved no more for it; Thomas and I together dwelt like souls in paradise.

Each morn we rose, very early, ate a little, and went out. Our dogs ran crazy with their freedom, round us and around. Poor beasts, we kept them close shut in with us, for some frenzy had possessed folk in the lower town, with fearing that dogs and cats, roaming free from house to house, carried the plague-seeds with them in their coats, and so the dogs and cats were caught and killed, leaving the children weeping for their favourites, and the rats having holiday. It was for their good that we let not Noll and Bess and Ranter freely roam, but how the poor things chafed, and scratched the door, and how we smiled to see them running free with us those mornings.

We moved our flocks to water, or to better grass, keeping ever within the bounds of Eyam, and seeing none but each other all the day. And I had winged feet all that time, like the heathen gods of Bradshaw's tapestries! At eve we came home again, and Thomas took a spade from by the door and went down to the parson's house, to find where the dead were lying, that he should bury that eve. And while he was gone I busied myself about the house, and set a supper cooking, and swept the floor, and smoothed the bed, and sang to myself, soft, under my breath. Then he would come home, and lean upon the doorpost, looking in at me.

He would be rimmed with gold, for the setting sun would catch upon his golden head and the red-gold hair upon his

125

wrists and arms, and bleach his shepherd's smock, and dazzle me. But though he stood in shade, or in rainlight, or in the summer darkness in the gardenside, I saw him always as apparelled in celestial light, and I warmed like a sunlit stone when he drew near me.

It was the fifth day of September, the first day when there were none to bury, for none had died. And then the eleventh, twelfth, thirteenth, fourteenth and fifteenth were likewise blessed. And there was news of the sick recovering, and in better numbers. Parson Momphesson, preaching in the Cucklett Church to his scattered and thinned people, told us it might yet abate and leave some of us living, as a fire that fiercely burns and consumes most of the coals, can leave some unconsumed, that are few enough and scattered. His words were cut short by a shower of rain, in which he would not for pity keep us standing long. And we in answer might well pity him, for he looked thin and haggard, and early old. He had a bandage about one of his calves, and there was some little stagger in his gait, as though he walked with pain.

'This must be over soon, if the parson is to weather it,' Mary Gregory said to me, as we came from the outdoor church.

'Which parson?' said I.

'Why, the old parson is like a rock, a crag. If it be true this is the Lord's punishment, which the virtuous should escape, then Thomas Stanley's virtue is plain to see. It is the new parson I mean. Poor gentleman, he hath overstretched himself, lost his wife, and spent all his strength in ministering to the sick. And all among a folk that like him not, and will barely afford him thanks!'

'Why surely, Mary, he is liked well enough by now...'

'He is even afraid for his wits, Mall. He told me so. He told me he had been making a will for Richard Talbot and he was so distracted he had written his own name in place of Goodman Talbot's, and had then to scratch it out. What-

126

ever people say against him, Mall, I will bear out he is a good and tender man, and kind to all, and kindest to the poorest.'

'But do folk speak against him, Mary?' I said, doubting her. It seemed to me it was Parson Stanley that had suffered exclusion and neglect. 'What can be said to reproach the new parson, leave aside matters of doctrine?'

'Why, some folk take it ill that he sent off his children to safety, when he would have others all caged in; and others take it ill that he did not send off that poor girl, his wife.'

'This is absurd,' I said.

'He is hated, Mall, because he is well. All we living hate each other for the sake of the dead.'

'He looks not well, to me.'

'No. He is even so not so hated as are you!'

'Me?' I said, standing heart-stopped where I stood.

'You are not only well, but happy, Mall Percival. An affront to all around you, in their grief.'

'But you, Mary, you think not so?'

'Why should I not?' she said. 'Is not my Robert dead and cold?'

'Ah, friend, I did not know! Alas, poor Mary, give me your hand . . .'

As we stood hand in hand there in the street, Agnes Sheldon overtook us. 'A pretty sight,' she said. 'A pretty sight, my maids. Hiding pits of iniquity, I doubt not! Whited sepulchres, the pair of ye! I pry, and pry, and yet some wickedness escapes me! As for thee, Mall Percival, I can make up an account against thee! But what thy mother did to deserve her death, I cannot find. What was it? Do you know? I'll guess at it, anon!'

I clenched my fist at her with the tears starting in my eyes, and Mary, still holding my hand, said, 'Forbear, Mall. She is surely cracked in her wits. Take no heed. We are all half crazed,' she added in a while, 'and should all keep our own counsel. Forgive me what I said, Mall.'

127

So I took my leave of her, and went home quiet and full of thought, and set about putting a rabbit to cook upon the spit, and to chopping the last few boughs of sage. Someone might yet have need of it. And now that Goody Trickett was lost, people came hoping to me, that I might know a little of what she knew. All my wisdom was sage tea; of that I made many pansful.

While I worked Thomas came in, and leaned, as was his way, upon the doorpost, and said, 'Sing me that air again, sweet Mouse.'

I looked up startled, and had nearly said, 'I sang not this while . . .' But then a deadly calm engulfed me, and I turned my face, as though to my task, and sang soft:

'For bonny sweet Robin is all my joy . . .'

'That's not it, Mall,' he said, smiling still. 'Tease me not. That air thou sangest a moment since, so sweet and sorrowful it would charm all the birds to hearken to it. I heard it all along the street as I came home to you. And now I would have it sung again, that I may listen close. Come, Mouse, come . . .'

'And it's all, all, all to plough,' I tried,

'Where the fat oxen graze, love;
'And the lads and the lasses to the sheepshearing go!'

'That's not it, yet, contrary wife!' he cried, protesting. 'Mock me not. Give me that air again, thou sangest just now!'

'Oh, Thomas, I don't know what it was!' I cried, and now he saw at last that something was amiss.

'Thou sangest . . . ?'

'Nothing.'

'I heard thee, Mall, sweet as a nightingale, drawing me home . . .'

Then in my mortal fear I ran to him, and clasped him in

my arms; and as I held him he winced, for a soreness that had come under his arm.

Do not the parsons also say that flesh is grass? That this is a Vale of Tears in which we dwell, and no joy, no delight, on earth endures? And in that saying they are right, are right! Thomas had caught the Plague, and, six days after, died of it. I have written elsewhere how the Plague goes. Thomas had all of it to suffer, which he did patiently for the most part. And when the fever broke he had a few hours lying calm and quiet, and I implored him to keep still, and not move a muscle for his life, and as he loved me.

'As I love thee is not still and quiet, Mouse, but lustily, come hither!' he answered, jesting, and reached out to me, and would have drawn me down to him . . . and as he stretched his arm, and grasped at my hand, his eyes emptied, and he was gone, like a candle going out in a gust.

Someone came in to take and bury him, I scarcely know. I know not who, or when. I took the sheet from off the empty bed, and brought it down the stairs. My guilt was dreadful to me, for it was my lying message that had entrapped Thomas, and brought him to his death. I had encompassed the last thing in the world I would have done. So I wrapped myself in the fouled bedsheet, and sat down in a chair in the middle of the room, and waited for the vengeance of the Lord.

The Lord our God is a harsh and a cruel God. How terrible the punishments he visited on the small sins of Eyam! Where was his mercy, when my neighbours died in torments for the theft of a thimble, or a wayward thought, or a careless unkind word! And I, who had sinned indeed, had lied, and lied to trustful, candid Thomas, and so brought about his death – would the providence of an affronted God not then bring death to me? The Lord God sees into our innermost hearts. The Lord God withheld his hand from punishing me in my death, since a more terrible punishment by far would be my life.

I sat long in melancholy, in a dark despond. How long I know not, but days and nights, while the dogs starved and whined at my feet. At last I got up, my limbs leaden, so heavy it was all I could do to shift myself a yard. I whistled to Noll and Bess their notes for running home to Wardlow, and they went. Ranter looked hopefully at me, and then slunk back in again, as I returned in silence to my chair. But I left the door wide; sometime he left, going to find food, surely. I marked not his coming or his going, but somewhere in those days he came not back to me, a neighbour having found him, and hanged him with a running noose about his neck upon the gate-tree.

Both parsons in that time came in to me. Parson Stanley prayed with me a while, or rather prayed beside me, for I said not a word. 'The Lord sees you, my child,' he said, at last.

'The Lord strike me down then!' I said.

'Speak not so. Have faith in your Saviour.'

'My wickedness mightily exceeds my faith,' I told him. 'Ask Agnes Sheldon. She will tell you.'

'Agnes Sheldon is dead, child. Yesterday.'

I laughed then, and said, 'Serves her right!'

'God serves us all right in his own good time,' he said, and left me.

Parson Momphesson came in and took away the bed-sheet with the stain and stench of Thomas on it that I had draped about me, and burned it in the grate. 'Get up, and wash thyself, and find something to eat,' he said.

'Why should I trouble?' I said. 'I am to die.'

'Have you the signs of it, Mall?' he asked.

I shook my head. 'Only my wickedness.'

Then he drew up a stool beside my chair, and took my hand. 'It may be, some day, there will be a physic found for

Plague,' he said. 'And will God's will then cease to be done? Doubtless God wills all things, but it is not for us to know his reasons, or his way of working. As he hath reminded us in the Bible, we were not there when he laid the foundations of the earth . . . If you are not sick, Mall, you are well. Get up and wash, for very shame!'

He went then to the door, but as he stood with his hand upon the latch already, he said, 'What would thy mother say, to see her kitchen thus?'

Then I got up, like a dead thing, and washed myself, and began to clean the house, and set the room to rights, from top to bottom. The labour made me faint, so I found a hardened crust of bread, and soaked it in cold sage tea to soften it, enough to eat it. And then I sat down in the chair again, and waited for the dust to fall again and lie, that I might have occasion to get up and clean it.

It takes a long while for the dust to lie heavy on a sill in a room where no one stirs. I think I had cleaned the house three times when Parson Momphesson came in to me again.

'Why do I live?' I asked him. 'Even my dog is dead. They have killed my dog.'

'You are too late,' he said. 'None has died since the eleventh of this month. And tomorrow November begins.'

'Why do I live?' I said, dully.

'Who can tell, child? I too have longed for my translation to a better place. We cannot know why we few are saved. But I conclude it is the prayers of good people that have rescued me from the jaws of death. I had been in the dust by now, I think, had not Omnipotence itself been conquered by holy violence!'

'For you; but who would pray for me?'

'I cannot tell that, either, child,' he said.

There came a time when the silence of the street, and the stillness of my quiet house, was suddenly broken by bells. A

131

great clamour of bells, ringing round all the slopes of Eyam, with brazen voices, shouting joy. The first and third and fourth of Eyam bells are marked 'Jesu be our speed'. The second says, 'God save the church'. And now all four clanged all together out of order, sang that the Plague was gone, gone, gone, gone, gone!

Then came I out into the untrodden street, and looked at Eyam with astonishment. In the clear cold of autumn no smoke from any chimney rose in view. The wide street was grassed over, side to side, with but a track winding down it, such as lovers make, walking through the corn. Across the doors the nettles grew thick and tall; and all along the banks of Fiddler's Brook, and by the stream where we all got our water, the rank leaves of marsh marigold, untrodden, promised a golden spring. I walked down Eyam street like a stranger, as though I looked upon it as had seen it never before, and came to Sydalls' house, of which the door stood wide, with coltsfoot growing free upon the threshold. I stepped within, staring all around. Grass grew up through each chink between the floor-flags; the pewter plates and pans were tarnished dark, the kettle flecked with rust, and in the garden windows spiders spun screens of web all thick with dust. The rain through the cold chimney had wet the hearth-stone, greening now with moss, and the linnet lay dead in its hanging wicker cage.

Out walked I again, and saw up the empty street, all loud with churchbells, someone coming, coming fast. Roland coming. I shrank to think of his question. I stood back, behind a tree. But before Roland drew nigh my hiding-place, a small boy running from his garden gate cried loudly to him, 'Roland! Thy Emmot's dead, and buried in the Cussy Dell!'

Roland sank down, and laid his face into his hands, there in the street; and I turned round and took myself home again, without word spoken. My dead heart could not pity him.

It was a time of fires, next. In the soft mists of morning, the bright flames, and the scorched smells of burning cloth. Parson Momphesson laboured to make us burn our clothes. His own he burned till he had scarce a shirt to stand up in, by way of example. He and his helpers took the torn and faded washing, left by dying housewives on the hedges, and every blanket in town, leaving us shivering day and night. They put a torch to the plague-huts on the common, and from the caves and summer-houses called the people home. Eliza and Bridget came within my house and took all my apparel, almost to my skin. They found within a chest a dress laid by five years, that I had well outgrown and never seen since, and put it on me; and it fitted my wasted form, and buttoned up. And on the fire every new dress went, every ribbon and lace, and fancy pinafore, and all we standing plain and puritan again!

John Merril, who had gone with his cock, and dwelt upon Sir William Hill without seeing a single soul, so far he did not even hear the bells, found his cock flew off and did not return; then followed he, and found the cock in his old quarters in Merril's yard, and the danger all passed by. Matthew Mortin at Shepherd's Flat saw his greyhound go and follow a woman walking along the Ridge; then thought he that the dog mistook her for his dead wife, and must see some likeness in her; so he went after Sarah Halksworth – for it was she walking there – who had been widowed in the first week of the Plague, and will have her to wife as soon as may be decent. I sold all Thomas's sheep, and all my own, to a man from Grindleford, who took advantage and paid but a poor price, but I had not heart to bargain better. A child died of the spotted fever in the Water Lane cottages just before Christmas, and two dozen funeral cakes were enough for us all.

Thus in such dull and small particulars crept time by. I went to the vestry once, to see the date of Thomas's death writ down, that I might mark time forward from it, like a stone that one paces away from on the upland runs ... I found his name only, with a handful of others, on the page marked 'October', but no dates set down. The parson had by then lost heart for the task, I supposed. Near to the last, the names had dates beside. And of our Eyam's sometime some three hundred and fifty souls, there were written the names of two hundred and sixty-seven dead, from George Vicars's name, 7th September 1665, until the names were written with no dates, in October 1666.

It was in the first days of the New Year, that Francis came to find me. 'We drag out but a broken-backed life here, Mall,' he said. 'Let me take you away.'

'Away, Francis?' I said, not understanding him.

'So far away from Eyam that it will baffle memory.'

'A foreign land?' I said, shaking my head. 'How would we fare in a foreign land?'

'But, Mall, there is another England, far away. A place in the New World, wherein is sweet English spoken, and a godly church endures, pleasant for Puritans. I have a friend there. A grant of land, he writes, may be had by such as we, sufficient for a farm; our house we must build, and the land we must clear, by our own labour ... dost thou heed me, Mall?'

'I can go nowhere with you, Francis,' I said.

'Thou must wed me first, Mall, true enough.'

'Begone, Francis!' I said. 'I can love never again. And if I could, you would be the last of many in my mind...'

'I know that, Mall. Yet hear me out. As you to Thomas, I for many years to you. I would not have spoken of it while Thomas lived. Come with me, and there may grow some liking between us, at the least; I would rather be at your side, Mall, every day, than parted from you, though every day you should hate me!'

'I do not hate you, Francis,' I said.

*

So Francis and I were wed with every living soul in Eyam to see it sworn, and the church but a quarter full. Yet was I loth to journey away with him.

'I am afraid of the sea, Francis,' I told him, seeking for a cause for my heaviness. 'What is the sea like? Is it not terrible to behold?'

Then Francis took my hand, and walked with me out of Eyam, and on the Wardlow road, where Thomas had once promised to be waiting for me, an old man; and across the upland and till we climbed Eyam Edge. 'Look at this land, Mall,' Francis said. 'The crests and dips, rolling as far as we can see, the softly swelling heights, and gentle vales. The sea is like this, only made all of water, as this of rock.'

'But is it smooth, and wide, and calm, Francis?'

'The waves do break upon it, Mall, into a flower of foam, like the long hedge of hawthorn breaking white in May, or the white weeds thick in flower at the lane-side in June.'

'Doth it sound like a brook, Francis?'

'Think of the strong wind blowing in the top of the trees,' he said. 'It sounds like that. There is danger in the sea, Mall, but it will not frighten thee. Thou wilt fear it no more than we fear this mountain land, because it lifts the heart to see it.'

I had never known that Francis had a way with him for words. 'I would like to see it,' I said.

But even so, when we began our ride-away to Whalley Bridge, and thence to Liverpool, and ship for America, I stopped in a mile and could go no more, because of voices. And there was Alice Sydall, and Emmot Sydall, and Ann Trickett, and Francis Archdale, and John Stanley, and Abel Coale, and Randol Daniel, and Mary Gregory, all being children of Eyam. All along the road I heard the voices of the dead, like children crying, calling after me, because once we played together . . . only when we turned for home did peace fall, and quietness.

Three times we tried it, on different roads. Always the voices stopped me. And yet when we were back, the melancholy once again engulfed me, and I sat down for days, and would not move nor speak.

At last Francis came to me, and said, 'Do you remember, Mall, a moonlit night, long since, when I stood by, while you made a charm for Eliza Abel?'

'Yes, I remember that. You were not supposed to hear.'

'And it was a ridding charm – a simple for heart's sorrow?'

'Yes.'

'And how did it work, Mall? What had to be done?'

'You must name the source of trouble, carefully writing down the cause of grief upon a paper. And when it is written down, you put it from you, in the fire, or in the back of the cupboard, or the bottom of the chest . . . and it carries away with it whatever is written thereupon.'

'How did it for Eliza?'

'Well, as I think.'

'Then listen, love. Tomorrow I will bring thee a book of paper that I have, with but two pages used. You shall write down all this whole doleful history that has befallen us, every name, every misery. All those voices that speak to you from aback you shall write down, and every memory that bruises your sore-troubled heart. Wilt thou do this for me? Then, when we go, we'll leave the book behind!'

This charm hath taken me full nine weeks to contrive. With tears and with difficulty have I written it all, set down as best I might, and as it came to mind, all that I know, or that anyone told me. This long while hath Francis tended me, bringing me food and drink, and trimming the candle when I wrote at night. And now, at last, it is brought to a conclusion. I shall lay it in my mother's linen chest, where let who may find it. It will lie heavy enough on the heart of who may read it, but writing of it has lightened mine!

Tonight I will close the book, and lay it in the chest, and go my way. Tomorrow Francis takes me with new heart, to a new home, new hope, New England!

And may God better understand and love us, than we, in our weakness, can do him.

AUTHOR'S NOTE

The villagers of Eyam in Derbyshire caught the Plague from a parcel of patterns sent from London, and eventually isolated themselves voluntarily for the sake of others, exactly as this book relates. The larger part of the story, with many of the smallest and some of the strangest details, is from the history and traditions of Eyam. Mall Percival and Thomas Torre are imaginary.

For particular help with this book I owe thanks to Betty Levin, shepherdess; to Clarence Daniel, scholar of Eyam; to John Townsend, for first telling me about Eyam, and for much other help; and to Marni Hodgkin, as much as ever.

J. P. W.
1982